"Who are you?" she whispered, her eyes full of wariness, of dread. "What are you?"

He sighed, leaning back in his chair and folding his arms across his chest. "I'm an architect," he admitted quietly.

Claire blanched. "And all this time you've been prowling around my house—spying!—looking for all the flaws, no doubt." Her voice trembled with mingled hurt and anger. "I'm surprised you even condescended to ask a lowly little home designer out for a meal. Did it give you a thrill to—"

"You know better than that," he cut across her diatribe, and although his voice was not raised, the authoritative ring silenced her. "I stopped at the house because I was interested in the design—it's an unusual one I hadn't seen before . . . I found the house, and then you, to be intriguing, and I wanted to see more of both . . ."

A SONG IN THE NIGHT

Sara Mitchell

Serenade/Serenata
B O O K S
of the Zondervan Publishing House
Grand Rapids, Michigan

A Note From the Author:
I love to hear from my readers! You may correspond with me by writing:

Sara Mitchell
1415 Lake Drive. S.E.
Grand Rapids, MI 49506

A SONG IN THE NIGHT

Serenade/Serenata are published by the Zondervan
Publishing House. 1415 Lake Drive. S.E.,
Grand Rapids, Michigan 49506

ISBN 0-310-47712-3

Edited by Lynda S. Parrish
Designed by Kim Koning

Printed in the United States of America

86 87 88 89 90 91 92 / 10 9 8 7 6 5 4 3 2 1

*In memory of my grandmother,
who provided almost 92 years
of inspiration.
And to my daughters,
who inherited her unquenchable
spirit and selfless love.*

You kept my eyes from closing;
*   I was too troubled to speak.*
I thought about the former days,
*   the years of long ago;*
I remembered my song in the night.
*   My heart mused and my spirit inquired:*
Will the Lord reject us forever?

Psalm 77:4–7 NIV

CHAPTER 1

SHE NOTICED THE CAR for the first time on a cloudy Tuesday evening. The sun was just setting over a restless Pacific Ocean, and the early April air was brisk with a promise of rain. It rained a lot around here in the spring, Claire Gerard was thinking as she paused from her labors to watch the red-orange sun sink behind a barrier of murky gray clouds that blended at the horizon with the ocean. From her vantage point at the second story window she could tell that the front was probably moving this way. "So much for sailor's delight," she muttered aloud, eyeing the vivid splash of vermilion. "With the way this house is going up it will probably rain for the next three days and put Chuck behind another week."

Chuck Degato was the contractor who had built the last two houses Claire had designed. He was a competent builder, but lousy at public relations. When weather or delayed shipments or some other cause set construction time back and the disgruntled homeowners-to-be came to Chuck, he irritably waved them on to Claire.

She sighed now, wearily shoving an errant lock of honey-toned hair out of her face. That was when she saw the car. It was a vintage '57 Thunderbird, restored in an unusual but eye-catching shade of burgundy. With a low growl the engine shifted to a lower gear. The car hovered in the middle of the street momentarily, then sped off with the deep purring roar of a well-tuned piece of machinery. Claire stared after it, frowning, wondering if the driver had liked the lines of the house as much as she had been drawn to the lines of the sleek, elegant car. She shrugged, realizing that her fame was spreading slowly but surely, and the time had passed when she had to hold her breath every time someone expressed the slightest interest in a home she had designed. Dream Designs was barely a year old in this small but well-known California community, but Claire could pay all her bills.

That night she sat down at her huge cherry desk to mull over a slight change she wanted to suggest to Chuck and the Mackleroy's before the workers started dry-walling. Large scrolls of paper, some rolled, some opened and curling on the ends, were scattered in apparent disarray over the surface of the desk. Several pencils, a ruler, two sizes of triangles, and a stack of other templates added to the clutter. Claire spread the plan of the Mackleroy's house over the top of everything, her slender fingers tracing lines as her hazel eyes narrowed in concentration. She had learned years ago that unless she was able to show, through her blueprints as well as verbal persuasion, that some of her less than standard ideas would work, the older male contractors would gently patronize her and build the houses as they saw fit.

After an hour she lifted her head, rotating it slowly to work out the kinks. She stretched her arms before her, and the glow of the desk lamp caught her ringless fingers. The pale mark on the fourth finger of her left hand was gone now, and her hands looked the same as they had ten years ago, when she was young and twenty and life was just beginning . . .

She saw the burgundy Thunderbird again the next afternoon. Rain was falling in a soft mist and there was no splashy sunset to accent its rich color, but the sound of that motor was unmistakable. Today Claire was downstairs in the area that would become a small formal living room, her hands balled into white fists at her sides. Chuck had just left after a frustrating confrontation. He would not widen the window sills. If Reba Mackleroy wanted a place to set her plants she could buy a table, or shell out the extra bucks he would demand to make the necessary changes. The Mackleroy's were not willing to do that, and Claire had had to let her idea die.

She had been standing there, picturing the huge bay window with a wide enough ledge for violets and philodendrons and maybe some impatiens, when she heard the subtle roar of the T-bird. It down-shifted again, then idled, but just as she moved over to peer out the window the driver pulled away and disappeared down the street. Claire could just make out the deep wine-colored finish, and she wondered who it was that could own a car like that but still be interested in a fourteen hundred square foot cottage that had taken the life savings of the Mackleroy's to build. Her unsmiling mouth barely tilted at the corner. The Mackleroy's drove a battered Chevrolet that could use a paint job.

They had been ecstatic over Claire's reasonable rates, pleased with the site they had found, and since their grown children only visited twice a year or so, the size of the house was more than adequate to meet their needs. Claire wondered what it would be like to have been married to someone for twenty-seven years. They seemed happy enough, but you could never tell. No, you could never tell.

She spent the next several days working in her office and prowling around the lot chosen by a brash young car salesman and his new wife, trying to come up with a design that met their specifications as well as fit on the narrow strip of land. You could see the Pacific, it was true, but there were no trees, for it had been a vacant lot used as a dump for years. Even the wealthy community of Pacific Grove had its eyesores. But Hal Redding had picked it up for "a song," and they could always plant trees. Claire had nodded and kept out of his way while he and his wife perused the stock designs she kept on hand. She was not surprised when they chose one of the modified A-frames.

Sunday was clear and warm with a prevailing wind off the ocean that filled the air with sea breezes and the sound of gulls. In the early afternoon Claire drove slowly out to the Mackleroy's house, along the narrow road that wound its way toward Monterey. On the way she passed by a church, and a twinge of remorse prickled through her, for she had not attended services since she moved out here from Georgia. Her parents would be hurt, but Claire could not explain the emptiness she felt, the alienation. They would never be able to understand, and Claire loved them both too much to give them more cause to worry than she already had.

She tossed her head, reached to turn on the radio, and forced her thoughts back to her eagerness to see what had been done to the Mackleroy's house. She realized that, as a home designer, officially her job had finished when she turned the completed set of prints over to Chuck. But she had never been able to turn loose that easily, and over the years, had ended up spending almost as much time at the site as she did designing her homes.

The only builder who had ever really understood, bless his indulgent old soul, was Mr. Jack. He had taught her a great deal about the actual construction of all the detailed lines she drew on paper. Consequently Claire had acquired a rudimentary but sound knowledge of plumbing, wiring, and construction that had ultimately served to increase the validity of her reputation.

Back in the small, tradition-bound community of Cherry Creek, Georgia, few people wanted to believe that little Claire had been trained—and had a degree to prove it—to design homes. That was one reason why, when Gary had seemed so supportive—so proud of her ability—Claire had ignored her mother and father's warnings about his background and the difference in their ages . . .

All the inadequacies oozed up again, like a slimy, evil-smelling mud that sucked at her tenuous tranquility. Her foot unconsciously jamming on the accelerator, hands clutching the wheel in a death grip, Claire arrived at the site of the Mackleroy's house in a frenzied rush, demons snatching at her like darting bats. Sitting out front was the burgundy Thunderbird, its sleekly waxed finish gleaming in the sunlight. Claire brought her cream Toyota to a skidding halt behind it, her heart lurching in a single spasm of nervous dread before she opened her door and gracefully got out. There was nobody inside the Thunderbird, which meant they must be wandering around inside the house. Claire stared up at the skeletal frame, noting almost absently that the bottom story was almost completely filled in with the sheathing now. Chuck's crew had accomplished a fair amount in spite of three days of rain.

She looked up as a man appeared at what would be the front door, and in spite of herself, stepped back.

"Hello, there," he called out in a friendly voice, stepping with careless grace over stacks of board, pieces of sheetrock, and several drying-up mud puddles as he moved down toward her.

Claire stared at him, her face not reflecting his easy

smile and friendly manner. "What are you doing here?" she asked, her voice neutral. She looked him over, noting the conservative but well-fitting light blue suit and the colorful navy and red striped tie he had loosened, revealing a strong-looking neck and sprinklings of curling black hair. His head was covered by more of that black hair, although it was more shaggy than curling, tousled even more by the wind and the hand that he was running through it at the moment. She could see by now that his eyes were a light, clear shade that was neither gray nor blue. Right now they were smiling directly into her face, and she felt hot, betraying color flood her cheeks.

"I take it I've been trespassing?" He grinned, unrepentant. "You're going to have a nicely designed house here, aren't you?"

"Yes. Thank you." She stepped toward the house and around the man. He was not a hulking giant, in fact he was a few inches shy of six feet. But the breadth of shoulder and lean, well-knit limbs spoke of strength and power, and Claire wanted no part of him.

The man turned with her. "I hope you don't mind that I looked around. I've been driving by since construction was started and I'm afraid my curiosity got the better of me."

"I've seen your car," Claire blurted out like a fool. She made her way back up to the house, her back straight and rigid. She knew he was following behind her, but she could not very well order him off the premises. How on earth would she carry out such an order?

"I drive this way to work every day," the man offered easily. He had stuffed his hands inside the waistband of his slacks, and was looking around with appreciation. "My name, by the way, is Elliot Ramsey."

"Mr. Ramsey." Claire nodded to him, about to utter some conventional remark when her eye caught on a newly placed wall switch. "Oh, that dratted electrician! The plans very plainly show the switch-plate on the *right* wall going into the kitchen." Without another glance toward Elliot Ramsey she stalked through the rest of the downstairs rooms, checking to see if any more light switches had been wrongly placed.

"Well, you've caught it early enough to fix things without undue delay," he commented, watching her with an unnerving look of stillness.

"I know that," Claire all but snapped. "But now I'll have to go home and call the contractor, and then the electrician because I can't depend on the contractor to take care of it himself." She stopped. Why was she explaining to this strange man, even if he had introduced himself?

"You might have trouble getting hold of them today. It's Sunday, you know." His gaze seemed to flick over her casual slacks and blouse, and Claire felt suddenly defensive.

"From what I've seen that doesn't seem to matter much anymore, especially out here. Sunday is just another day."

"Is that how you feel about Sundays?" he inquired without any hint of censure, but Claire bristled anew.

"Look, Mr. . . . Ramsey. I don't know you, and I would feel a lot more comfortable if you would—if you would—" She tried to frown, but it was difficult when that indulgent grin spread across his face and his eyes seemed to sparkle like silver fire.

"If I would mind my own business, and disappear?" he finished for her, the smile deepening along with Claire's guilty blush. "Anything for the uptight lady with the beautiful green eyes." He lifted his hand in a wry gesture of farewell, then wandered outside with the careless grace of a sleek cougar. Claire was still standing where he had left her when he called back through the open doorway. "See you around.

Just remember, today is supposed to be a day of rest."

As he drove toward his apartment Elliot found himself dissecting every strange moment spent in the company of the woman he had just left. She had acted like a wary mother cat defending a litter of kittens, and he had to smile over her possessiveness. Most women could care less about the messy construction phase of their homes. But this young woman—well, she didn't look all that young, either, and the shadows beneath her eyes and the lines on her forehead hadn't helped—had gazed at the half-finished house as if it were her pride and joy. Elliot shook his head in rueful understanding. He could understand feelings like that since he was an architect by profession and had doubtless exhibited the same feelings himself for the scores of buildings he had designed and watched take shape.

Why had she been so hostile? He might not be a Robert Redford or a Burt Reynolds, but he wasn't used to such a negative reaction from a woman. *Yeah, Lord, I hear You. Let's watch it in the self-importance category.* She hadn't just been hostile, though. He pulled into his driveway and switched off the ignition absent-mindedly, his eyes seeing a fragile woman of average height who looked like she was nothing but skin over delicate bones, held together by tension. And the way she had glided so deliberately out of his reach, almost as if she were—yes, afraid. Beneath the cool disdain, the chilly politeness, even the show of frustration and flustered embarrassment, there had hovered a shadowy specter of . . . fear. She had been so tightly controlled, though, so obvious about her dislike of his presence, that the other emotion had only registered subliminally until now.

Who *was* she? He had not seen any rings, but she could still be involved with a man. Somehow that realization was depressing, and Elliot grimaced as he let himself into the double-sized apartment he had designed for his own use. He didn't know her name, where she came from, what she did, or if some two-hundred pound jock was waiting in the wings, but he was going to pursue her all the same. *I still hear You, Lord, but You know Yourself how it goes . . . 'the way of a man with a maiden,' remember? I promise to proceed carefully, though. She looks as if anything else would send her running the other way.*

For three days Claire slunk around the Mackleroy's house like a furtive rat watching for a cat. She always timed her visits early, or just before dusk, in the hopes that Elliot Ramsey would not find her again. She had lectured herself severely and had almost succeeded in shrugging the episode aside. Then, on a gilt-edged, breezy morning, she caught the plumber as he was about to install pipes of the wrong material.

"The specs plainly state copper instead of PVC," she argued with thinning composure.

"I saw 'em." The plumber casually chewed a minute on the plug of tobacco couched in his cheek, then just as casually spat onto the plywood subflooring. Claire winced, but gamely kept her eyes on his face. A spare, weathered man with an enormous pot belly, Mr. Rodriguez wearily scratched his bristled chin, then chewed on his plug another minute. "Mr. Degato like the PVC better. He's the builder, so I use PVC."

"Cooper is better," Claire stated flatly. She glanced at her watch. "It's only a little past seven-thirty. I'll go and call Mr. Degato and straighten this out. Is there anything else you can be doing? It shouldn't take me but ten minutes or so—there's a convenience store a mile down the road where I can use a phone."

"Well, now . . . I've got another job down at Carmel this afternoon. Are you going to explain to

Mr. Degato if I can't finish here this morning?" He spat again, shrugging his stooped shoulders and looking faintly apologetic.

"Good morning," came Elliot Ramsey's cheerful baritone voice, and Claire whirled around with a gasp. Her heel caught on one of the scattered pieces of pipe and his hand shot out to steady her.

Claire pulled free the moment she recovered her balance. "You startled me," she accused him, smoothing her hands over her jeans and avoiding the piercing directness of his stare.

"I'm sorry." He glanced over at Mr. Rodriguez, shaking his head ever so slightly as the plumber looked like he was going to speak. "Is anything else the matter?"

"No." Claire shot the plumber a determined look. "I was just leaving, as a matter of fact." She moved around Elliot with the same dainty care she had used the other day, gazing up through thick brown lashes as she passed. "I hope you won't be late for work," she tossed back pointedly, and then she was outside and scurrying down to her car.

When she returned some twelve minutes later the rakish little T-bird was still there, mocking her with its presence. Claire sighed, wondering if the ubiquitous Elliot Ramsey would be rude enough to stand there while she was forced to eat crow. Chuck would not budge on his preference for PVC, and Claire had had to yield. She swallowed hard, lifted her chin, and marched up the slight slope and inside the house. Mr. Rodriguez and Elliot Ramsey were upstairs, their voices filtering down clearly through the studs and enclosed stairwell. Mr. Ramsey was laughing, and Claire felt a strange shivering as if something warm and fuzzy had tickled her spine.

"Ah, I thought I heard you." Elliot's head appeared, followed by the rest of him as he descended the staircase. The genuine admiration in his eyes was

16

so blatant that Claire gaped up at him. "Mr. Rodriguez has been telling me about you." He lifted his hand as if to touch her, then withdrew it. He casually maneuvered so he was standing between Claire and a wall that had been enclosed in the silvery sheathing. "I found out you're not an eager homeowner after all. You're the designer of all the homes *for* the eager homeowners."

Claire, her heart beating so fast she felt light-headed, kept her gaze focused over Elliot's shoulder, on a bent nail hammered into a stud. "Yes," she admitted. "I am a home designer. Did you perhaps want to use my services, Mr. Ramsey? Is that why you act so interested in this house?"

The strangest expression went washing over his face, only to be replaced by an even more puzzling expression of tender amusement. "I act interested because I *am* interested," he reprimanded her very gently. "And no, I'm not in the market for a house right now, but you can rest assured that if I ever am, I'll let you know." He turned as the plumber cleared his throat loudly, descending the stairs with heavy tread.

"Mr. Rodriguez," Claire squeezed past Elliot in a flurried little rush, gesturing to the plumber with fluttering fingers. "Could I speak to you a moment, please?" She glanced back at Elliot. "If you wouldn't mind . . ."

"I was just going." He watched her a moment, holding her trapped within the compelling confines of his light-emitting eyes. "I'll be seeing you, Claire Gerard."

Well, she hadn't told Mr. Rodriguez not to blab her name and any other information, Claire kept reminding herself through the rest of the day. She found herself on several different occasions staring into space, pencil suspended in hand and the half-finished plans lying forgotten on her desk. Elliot Ramsey had unnerved her, and he couldn't possibly have any idea of the reasons why. She had hoped, after all this time, that she would have gotten better; but this morning, when she was trapped between his sinewy, solid body and the wall, it had been all she could do to keep from crashing through the far less solid sheathing. The pencil dropped from suddenly nerveless fingers as her eyes filmed over.

All the fear, all the hatred . . . all the mind-destroying guilt burst through the tightly closed lid of her memory, and with an incoherent cry she rose, snatched a sweater from the bentwood coat rack, and fled. The bulk of the afternoon she spent walking on the beach, wind whipping through her hair and sand filling her worn sneakers. By the time her antique mantel clock struck five she had returned, the lid to her memory once more secured and the only evidence of her restless soul the shadows in her gold-flecked hazel eyes.

The days passed and the Mackleroy's house continued to take shape. The sheathing was finished on both floors, and the insulation was almost in so that it was starting to look more like a real house. "Flesh and blood instead of just bones," Claire had joked one time, years ago. She didn't joke a lot anymore, but she stayed too busy to sigh over the carefree, guileless person she used to be. Not only had she landed the contract for the car salesman and his wife, but a couple who had moved down from Sacramento had seen the house she designed last year for some of their friends. They had been enthusiastic about her ideas for maximizing space while conserving costs, since they had four children and were watching every penny.

Elliot Ramsey probably didn't have to watch pennies. The intruding thought pricked like a pin, but Claire had learned not to fight such thoughts by now. She had almost grown accustomed to his frequent appearances at the Mackleroy's house, and he never stayed long enough to really intrude. He was polite, interested, knowledgeable . . . and he made her want to smile. Since that morning with Mr. Rodriguez he had not come close enough to make her uncomfortable, and since there were usually workmen milling and hammering and sawing there was no reason for her to be such a nervous Nelly. He seemed to like to stop on his way to work in the mornings, and Claire kept meaning to ask him what he did. She had found, to her annoyance, that when she avoided coming in the mornings, Elliot would stop by on his way home in the late afternoon, when most of the workmen had gone. Claire had tried staying away altogether, but could not, so she had given in and, to her utter astonishment, found that Elliot Ramsey was not such an ogre after all.

Then he invited her out to dinner.

"It's obvious you could use a good meal," he punctuated this unflattering remark by a swift but thorough examination of her person. "I'm hungry, you need a good meal, and it's—" he flexed his arm, reading the analog dial of a plain gold watch that probably cost as much as Claire's monthly rent, "going on six. Did you have plans for this evening?"

For years before she moved out here to California, Claire had lived with lying, with lies. She found now, staring up helplessly into those knowing eyes, that she couldn't lie to Elliot Ramsey. "N—no," she stammered. "But I—I'm busy," she finished on a triumphant note, relieved to have come up with such a reasonable solution. "I promised a couple that I would have the drawings of their house ready by Friday and—"

"Claire," he interrupted, his mouth firm and the smiling eyes serious, intent. "Come to dinner with me. I promise you'll enjoy it." He paused, then added deliberately, "And I also promise not to do anything to alarm, annoy, or upset you . . . such as making a pass, or even holding your hand. Okay?"

Color crept up her face, spreading from throat to hairline in a wave of shame. "What must you think of me?" she muttered miserably, wishing she could crawl under the stairs into the space reserved for the water heater.

He smiled then, a slow, gentle smile that managed to burn its way into her heart and lit a small flame. "I'll tell you what I think of you over dinner, Claire Gerard, although I will confess—upon penalty of jeopardizing the evening—that your blush is most becoming. I didn't think a woman your age would still know how."

"What do you mean, 'a woman of my age?' " She glared at him, shame forgotten, and Elliot laughed outright.

"I thought that would do it. Tell me, Ms. Gerard, just how old are you, anyway?"

"Don't you know that's the worst possible question you could ask any woman over twenty-one?" She itched to answer that bone-melting smile, but there had been too many years when she had had nothing to smile about, and it seemed her mouth had forgotten how.

"Vanity, vanity, all is vanity," Elliot quoted. "Don't you know you're not getting older, you're getting better?"

"I'm not that old!" Claire snapped. "I'm only thirty—" she clapped her hand over her mouth, eyes spitting mad as Elliot was convulsed in laughter. That sound was so pleasing, so contagious, that something inside her cracked, then melted, and her mouth spread in a wide, sheepish smile.

Elliot stopped laughing, and his eyes took on a deep blue hue as he stared at Claire's changed countenance. "Oh, my," he breathed as if awestruck, "when you smile you're devastating, did you know that?" As if with a will of its own his hand lifted to her face, and Claire flinched back, the smile wiped away with the abruptness of a pistol shot.

For a frozen moment they both stood there, then Elliot flicked back a wayward lock of his hair before dropping the hand once more to his side. "I know of a good seafood restaurant in Monterey," he spoke evenly, in an offhand manner as if nothing had happened. "Do you like seafood?"

Claire nodded, her eyes never leaving Elliot.

"Come along, then. We'll take my car and I'll bring you back here later." He waited for her to precede him, being careful to maintain at least three feet of space between their bodies.

"I really should go home," Claire tried feebly. Her hands were clammy and her heart was racing, but she knew Elliot knew there had not been any conviction in her statement.

"It's all right, little mouse," Elliot promised, his voice deep and incredibly tender. "Don't worry, it's all right."

They were at the cars now, and he waited by the passenger door of the Thunderbird. He hadn't touched her, hadn't come near her, but Claire felt as if she were a pebble tossed headlong into the current of a swift moving, bottomless mountain stream. Her movements slow but inevitable, she walked over and folded herself into Elliot's little car. The door shut with a solid thunk, but before the panic had time to rear its ugly head he had slid in beside her. His gaze reached across the small space separating them and seemed to caress her. "Claire . . . trust me," he said, the tones liquid, compelling.

"Why?" she asked, keeping her hands still in her lap, her back pressed rigidly against the plush gray leather seat.

Elliot paused in the process of turning the key. In the fading light the rays of the setting sun streamed

21

through the window, causing his hair to gleam like a raven's wing. The fingers poised at the ignition were long, supple, capable of great strength, but not once in the last weeks of their strange acquaintance had he tried to intimidate her with a show of that strength.

"I guess it's like my faith in God," he stated thoughtfully at last. "I know He could do anything He wanted to me, but because I've come to know His Son, and through Him, God Himself, I trust Him to take care of me." He glanced across at Claire.

"But that kind of relationship takes time, and I can see you and I need the same thing: time." Once again he smiled that slow, utterly devastating smile, and in spite of what she thought were insurmountable barriers, Claire found herself relaxing. "Let's get to know one another, Claire Gerard, and then I hope you won't feel the need to even ask that question."

CHAPTER 2

HE TOOK HER TO AN oceanfront restaurant with a walkway right over the water. A tuxedo garbed maître d' led them to a table for two by a window, and a waiter appeared immediately to present Elliot with a wine list. Elliot lifted a brow at Claire, who shook her head, and then politely declined for himself. As they looked over the menus, Claire found herself more and more fascinated by the man sitting across from her.

He acted so confident, so sure of himself, but with a disarming consideration for others she had never seen in a man before. And he made no apologies for his deep faith, nor did he come across as some pious, self-righteous fanatic. Claire wanted to ask him about his feelings, especially the words he had spoken just before they left the house.

Why was he so confident that God would never hurt him? He obviously had not been down the road Claire had traveled, and so God would have no reason to punish him. But He did have every reason to punish her, oh, yes, He did, and Claire woke every day with that dreadful knowledge.

"If it looks that bad maybe we better leave and try McDonald's."

Elliot's teasing voice intruded into her dismal reverie, bringing her back to the present with a jerk. "What?" She lifted puzzled eyes to him, then stared down at the menu she was holding.

"Your expression," Elliot explained, folding his menu to probe the features of her face as if he were holding a magnifying glass. "You looked unhappy, Claire, and I wondered if it was the menu . . . or something else."

There was a waiting quality in his stillness, but Claire could not answer the unspoken question. "The menu is fine," she assured. "I think I'll try the stuffed baked flounder." She had never had it before and had chosen the first thing her eye focused on.

Elliot watched her another minute. "It's supposed to be excellent," he concurred. "I like their seafood brochette marinade myself—there's just something about shish kebabs that appeals to me." He smiled across at her. "Maybe I should have been a fencing instructor."

When Claire merely gave him a polite little smile in return he mentally reminded himself not to probe too much too soon. "I understand you've been in California about a year now. Where did you come from?"

"Georgia."

Up went the slashing black eyebrow. "That's a long way, but at least it explains your charming accent. What made you uproot to become a worshiper of the Golden State?"

Claire shrugged, took a sip of the ice water from the clear crystal goblet. "Have you always lived here?" she countered, and earned a rueful grin from Elliot.

"Believe it or not, I am a native Californian. My parents wandered out here in the forties, after the war, and stayed. They still live in a house Dad built up in the Gold Country." He grinned reminiscently. "It's

24

a log cabin, plunked right on top of a hill in a stand of sugar pines, and I can't persuade either one of them to live out their 'golden years' in a more . . . civilized community." He looked across at Claire, but for the first time she felt he wasn't really seeing her.

"Mom said that until she goes to be with the Lord, she might as well be as close to Him on earth as she can get, and the Sierras is as close to heaven on earth as is possible." His eyes were brimming with love and tenderness, and Claire suddenly felt bereft and achingly lonely. What would it be like to have a man look at her like that?

"I can understand," Elliot ended the nostalgic recital, his gaze once again focusing on Claire. "In the last few years I've also discovered the magic of the Sierras." He nodded to the waiter who had just arrived to take their orders. "I'll explain why later."

While they waited for the meal Elliot entertained her with light conversation that was impersonal, nonthreatening, and designed to relax. He had almost succeeded in accomplishing this feat when a large, beefy man materialized beside them, his booming voice an unpleasant intrusion that sent Claire scurrying behind her formidable barrier of aloofness.

"Elliot! How ya' doing, old man?" He slapped Elliot heartily on the back, and winked across at Claire. "Say, I've been trying to get hold of you all week. Who's this sweet little number ya' got with you?"

With a resigned look Elliot introduced Claire, watching as she coolly kept his gregarious acquaintance at a safe distance by merely nodding regally, daring him with wide blank eyes to come any closer.

"Say, listen, Elliot." With clumsy movements he dragged out a chair and dropped into it. "I'll only be a minute, but while I got you, I'll take advantage." He chortled, and leered across at Claire. "I'm flying down to San Diego tomorrow—have an appointment with that contractor you hired to build the walkway for that hotel. I called your secretary this afternoon, but you were out at the site. Aren't you doing the First Federal Bank in Salinas? Anyway, I talked with Joe and he said the new specs for that walkway were ready, and since I was going down I told him I'd pick them up for you." He chortled again, rising to slap Elliot's back once more. "Now ya' owe me one, pal, right?"

Elliot was looking across at Claire, and his expression was grim. "I owe you, Solly," he replied evenly. "But not in the way you think." He tore his gaze away from Claire and looked up at Solly, whose already flushed countenance took on a deeper hue. Solly glanced across at Claire, who was sitting in frozen silence, mumbled an apology for intruding, and shuffled off.

"Claire—"

"Who are you?" she whispered, her eyes full of wariness, of dread. "What are you?"

He sighed, leaning back in his chair and folding his arms across his chest. "I'm an architect," he admitted quietly.

Claire blanched. "And all this time you've been prowling around my house—spying!—looking for all the flaws, no doubt." Her voice trembled with mingled hurt and anger. "I'm surprised you even condescended to ask a lowly little home designer out for a meal. Did it give you a thrill to—"

"You know better than that," he cut across her diatribe, and although his voice was not raised, the authoritative ring silenced her. "I stopped at the house because I was interested in the design—it's an unusual one I hadn't seen before."

He lifted his hand as she started to speak. "And before you accuse me of stealing, let me assure you that I very seldom design single dwellings anymore, and when I do they're usually between four and five thousand square feet." He leaned forward, planted his palms on the table and stared straight into her confused, hostile gaze. "I found the house, and then you, to be intriguing, and I wanted to see more of both. Claire, just because I'm an architect does not mean I have to pose a threat to you, or to your career."

Up went her firm little chin. "You're absolutely right. I'm doing quite nicely with my career, probably because I don't charge the exorbitant rates you do."

The corner of Elliot's mouth quirked, but before he could reply their food arrived. The waiter placed the steaming dishes in front of them. When they were alone again he deliberately took a few bites, savoring the aroma in spite of the fact that at the moment he might as well have been chewing seaweed. "I rather imagine I do charge more for my services," he murmured almost idly in between bites. "But as I'm sure you're well aware, my training is a little more extensive than yours, and as I said, I don't design many homes anymore."

"They're beneath your notice, I'm sure."

"Not at all." He kept his voice even, but the level gaze he shot at her was a reprimand. "I seem to have acquired something of a reputation for churches and commercial buildings, and just plain don't have time for the other."

Blast! That hadn't come out well and had made him sound like a prima donna. Sure enough, Claire dropped her fork, leaving the delicious-looking flounder untouched.

"Claire, eat your dinner and try to stop feeling so defensive and intimidated." He tried a placating smile. "I feel like there's nothing I can say right now that won't make matters worse. Let's enjoy the meal, and I promise to keep the conversation well away from any mention of our respective career fields. By the time you've tried a dessert from their pastry

27

trolley you'll realize we have more in common than you think.''

"We don't have anything in common," Claire retorted, her voice almost breaking. She dropped her gaze, toying with the silverware and not touching her food. The flounder might be splendidly prepared, a culinary delight, but her stomach was churning and the thought of having to eat was more than she could bear. What on earth had possessed her to order seafood anyway? And why had she even told Elliot she liked it? The only seafood to which she had ever been exposed had been frozen fillets and fishsticks at school years ago. Mom was a southern cook through and through, with meals that ran from fried chicken, rice and gravy, to pork roast and yams, to roast beef and mashed potatoes with turnip greens and summer squash . . .

I've got to get out of here. The words repeated themselves in a frantic refrain until she was numb from her toes to her panicking brain. He must think she was the most gullible, pathetic fool on the Pacific Coast. And to think he had had the gall to pretend admiration for her dinky little house! Oh, what was she thinking? She was *proud* of her accomplishments. She was talented, she had nothing of which to be ashamed . . . *I've got to get out of here.*

"Excuse me . . ." she pushed her chair back and rose with clumsy haste. "I'm not hungry. I'm sorry." She walked toward the exit, her mind whirling like a blender, jumbling all the thoughts and grinding them to incoherent fragments. She would go to the ladies' room . . . or she would find a phone and call a taxi.

His hand closed around her arm, and she jumped with the shock of it. "Claire," he spoke her name firmly but with an underlying note of gentleness. "Here—sit down and let's talk about it." Ignoring her frantic body language he guided her to a tufted velvet bench and sat her down, then joined her. He watched as she moved as far away from him as she could, his eyes narrowing as her hand came up to rub over and over the place on her arm where he had held her.

"There's nothing to talk about." Thank heavens her voice sounded so calm. He mustn't know—mustn't suspect how rattled she was. "You played a dirty trick on me for someone who claims to be such a committed Christian." Her eyes accused him briefly before seal-colored lashes swept down to veil her pain. "I apologize for spoiling your meal. Please go back and enjoy it—I was planning to call a taxi for myself. I–I'm not hungry."

"You're right. I should have told you. Will you forgive me?"

Her gaze flew upwards, her mouth dropping open at the low note of regret, the expression of pain on his face. There was no blue in his eyes now: in the dim lighting of the restaurant lobby they were almost smoky gray, like fog rolling in over Monterey Bay. He wasn't even trying to rationalize, explain away his deception, but just sat there waiting for her to say something. Claire was flummoxed. Every time Gary had apologized he had spent a good thirty minutes justifying what he had done. The lid on her memory strained against the encroaching thoughts, and it was all Claire could do to keep from blurting them out loud. "I—you, you're admitting you were wrong?" She had no idea of how incredulous she sounded, how stunned she looked.

"Is that so impossible to believe?" Elliot inquired, searching her bewildered, still wary eyes. "I know I should have told you the day I found out you were a home designer. But Diego Rodriguez, the guy doing your plumbing, told me you were pretty touchy." He smiled sheepishly then. "I've known Diego for years—he's even done some sub-contracting for me—and instead of going with my instincts I listened to him and kept quiet about who I was." He sighed. "You were already upset that morning, and I didn't want to make matters worse."

"Mr. Rodriguez thinks I'm touchy?"

Elliot leaned forward slightly, and Claire automatically shifted away. He lifted his hand, watching her eyes follow the movement and darken as he let it fall on top of her hands, held tightly clenched together in her lap. The jerk was spasmodic, involuntary, but this time Elliot did not release her.

"Actually, I think he meant you're just the opposite," he observed, his voice reflective. "You really don't like to be touched at all, or have anyone invade your space. Tell me something, Claire Gerard. Have you ever been married?"

"Is that any of your business?" Was that overused retort the best she could do? She summoned all her will power to ignore the warmth of that hand, the feeling of entrapment at the nearness of his body.

"I'd appreciate it if you would let go of my hand. You're absolutely right. I do not like to be touched, especially by arrogant men who try to pick at my brain like a bug under a microscope."

Somehow he managed to caress her hand as he released it. "Is that what you think I'm doing?"

She breathed a sign of relief, still unaware of the turmoil reflected in her eyes or the aura of finely wrought tension that radiated from her. "Aren't you?" Her voice was even again, thank heavens, and she could even meet his gaze with a modicum of composure.

"I'm going to have to let you decide that for yourself," Elliot told her without batting an eye. "A matter of trust, remember?" Then, so swiftly she did not have time to protest or react, he had drawn her to her feet. "Can you eat your supper or would you still prefer to go home?"

She could hear her mother's outraged scolding for

letting such an expensive meal go to waste, not to mention her unforgivable breach of manners to have left the table with her flimsy excuse. As long as Elliot kept his distance and made no further attempts to touch her, surely he could recover enough of her poise to keep from ruining her already tarnished image.

As if he could read her every thought Elliot spoke up beside her. "I'll leave you alone, Claire. I promise, even if it means forever earning my father's wrath for not holding your chair for you, since to do so I would have to—" he paused, his voice dropping to a husky whisper that sounded like a cat's purr, "—come close to you to do so."

"Don't be ridiculous," Claire returned tartly, but her mouth was still dismayingly dry. "I'm not some shy, simpering teenager, and just because I–I don't care to be pawed by a virtual stranger does not mean I would object to a basic show of courtesy."

He was laughing at her again, but Claire could also see that he was relieved. Did eating with her mean more than she had thought after all? His next ambiguous observation further confused her.

"Ah, good, the green's coming back. Come on, then, before everything is stone cold and the waiter glares at us unforgivably." He held up his hand, gesturing for her to precede him back into the dining room. He did not touch her.

Claire waited until they were seated again, snowy white linen napkins back in their laps and Elliot having assured the hovering waiter that no, nothing was wrong and they were fine. She picked up her knife and fork, cut a small piece of the flounder, then held it poised halfway to her mouth as curiosity got the better of her. "What did you mean by your remark?" she asked, watching the teasing glint catch fire and turn his eyes to molten silver.

"About what?" he asked innocently, applying himself with male heartiness to his meal.

31

Claire tried the flounder, grimacing before she could help it at the strange texture and taste. She gulped some water and then looked back at Elliot, who was watching her with an unnerving mixture of comprehension and tenderness. "That comment you made," she supplied hastily. "About their being back to green. What did you mean?"

"Oh, that. Your eyes." He speared a pineapple and popped it into his mouth. "Surely you've been told before how your eyes change color to reflect your emotions. You're an open book, Claire Gerard, and very easy to read." He smiled across at her, but Claire could not share in his wit. She looked stunned, dismayed.

"No . . ." she looked down at the flounder lying with the crabmeat stuffing oozing out in mouth-watering succulence as if she didn't see it at all, "no one has ever said anything like that to me." Least of all Gary, who hadn't even known her favorite color, much less what shade her eyes turned to reflect her emotions. But then, after only a short while she hadn't wanted him to notice her at all, and when he did he wouldn't have cared what emotion she might be revealing.

Only God knew what emotions she had gone through in those years, and at the thought, Claire cringed anew. One day He would wreak an even more terrible punishment on her, and she would deserve it. Yes, she would deserve it, but it didn't stop her from being afraid or dreading what she knew would eventually have to come.

"Hey . . . Claire. Claire!" His voice turned insistent, but when she lifted her head Elliot inhaled sharply. *God, what has happened to cause her to look like that? You're really going to have to help me this time, Lord, because I feel like I'm walking blindfolded through a minefield.* "Claire—" This time he spoke her name with petal-soft gentleness, "I think I'd do almost anything to keep that look from appearing on your face. Won't you tell me about it?" He sighed as he watched her fiddling with the now-mutilated fish. "You don't like that at all, do you?" he offered her the out, although at her giveaway blush he had to acknowledge that embarrassing her was not much kinder than pressing her about something that was obviously very private.

All Claire wanted to do was melt under the table and into discreet oblivion. She was thirty years old, had built up a successful career in home-designing, rebuffed countless men from fifteen to fifty, and yet Elliot Ramsey in the last hour had reduced her to a quivering mass of schoolgirl nerves. She couldn't even scrape together enough poise to fake polite enjoyment of her meal. "It's fine," she lied stiffly, and put another mouthful into her mouth.

Elliot watched her trying to pretend for a brief agonizing minute, then he lifted a hand to summon the waiter. "I'm afraid we have to leave," he informed the surprised man, folding his napkin and tucking it under his plate as he was talking. "Could you bring me the check, please?"

The waiter glanced at Claire's plate and his eyebrows rose. He was too well-trained to make a comment, although he did ask if they wanted dessert.

"Next time," Elliot promised.

Within five minutes they were walking back down the boardwalk, the weathered beams creaking pleasantly beneath their feet, waves slapping in lazy splashes against the barnacled support posts. It was almost dark, and a line of long, dark clouds blotted the sky, promising another day of rain tomorrow. Elliot nodded to a couple walking past them on their way into the restaurant, but he didn't speak. Neither he nor Claire said anything the whole way back to the site of the Mackleroy's house.

Claire was relieved at this. She had found out that this man for whom she had privately acknowledged a budding attraction was an architect, the one profession which had never had any pretensions as to their feelings for professional home designers. She had made a fool of herself at dinner, not only about the food, but about herself. She had no illusions about either her career or her personality, but to have exposed both in such an unflattering manner to Elliot Ramsey was a bitter pill to swallow. If he would only refrain from making any more trenchant comments she could escape to her car, and then home, where she could writhe in privacy and rebuild the barriers Elliot had started to tear down.

"I'll follow you home."

Claire gaped at him. She had been so intent on her escape that she had leaped out of the car without speaking the minute it stopped. Elliot had followed her, and she had not even been aware of it.

"That's not necessary," she fumbled in her purse for the keys. "And I feel I owe you an apology as well as a note of thanks for—for the dinner." Bravely she faced him as she finally located the keys and then unlocked her car door.

Elliot shrugged off the disaster of dinner. "I think most of it was my fault," he admitted wryly. "I am going to follow you home, however." When she started to speak he shushed her, his index finger barely brushing her lips. "I was taught early on to always escort the lady to her door. Not—" he amended with a swift grin as he blocked Claire's movement to swing shut the car door, "—this one, but the door to her home." He looked down at her a minute, head tilted to one side as if he were considering whether or not to make a comment.

Claire thought she had schooled her face to blankness, but Elliot must have seen something, for the grin faded to somberness. What was it he had said about the color of her eyes revealing her feelings?

"You don't know what to make of me, do you?" he commented with soft precision. "And every time I touch you, or even come too close, you act like a doe facing the barrel of a gun. I want to know why, Claire Gerard. I will know why, and I give you fair warning." He stopped, waited until he could see her full reaction to his statement. "I might have kept from you the fact that I happen to be an architect, but I have never lied to you. In my book—and in The Book—lying is considered a sin. One of the reasons is probably because it has a way of destroying trust, which destroys relationships between people, and I very much would like to pursue a relationship with you." He reached out and rolled down Claire's window, then shut the door as if he realized how much safer she felt with the layers of metal between them. "Is that honest enough for you?"

"A little too honest," Claire confessed, her own face pale, the hazel eyes huge and dark in the fading glow of dusk. "I don't want a relationship with a man, Elliot. Please leave me alone and let me drive myself home. Please." She hated to plead. She had promised herself she would never again plead with a man about anything.

Elliot closed his eyes briefly, an expression of deep weariness and frustration etching deep grooves in his forehead, from nose to cheek. "I can't," he ground out. He stepped back, looked up toward the heavens as if speaking to the Lord Himself. "I can't," he repeated, and there was a strangled note of agony in his voice. The he turned and strode with swift steps over to the Thunderbird.

Claire started her own car automatically, her gaze still on Elliot, her ears still hearing the desperation in his impassioned denial. Fear coiled around her heart in choking ropes, but there was another emotion along with the fear that she didn't analyze. She couldn't. It was excitement, tinged with anticipation, and she had

35

felt neither for so long she was not aware of feeling them now.

As she drove slowly home, ever aware of the headlights in her rearview mirror, she could only wonder if Elliot would truly see her to the door, or just drive away into the night with a careless wave. If he saw her to the door, would she invite him in?

No man had been inside her home since she moved here. Plenty had seen her office, of course, which was the two front rooms of the house she had leased, but it had been in a business capacity. She had no desire to ever again cope with the demands of establishing a relationship with a man. Not only was the effort too painful, but in her case there was the bitter knowledge that she did not have the right.

Mom and Dad had tried to tell her she would feel differently after awhile. All she needed was time. There were other men in the world, other men who would be just as nice as Gary had been. Claire had almost screamed out on those occasions. Mom, Dad, you were right about him all along! Why can't you see as clearly now?

Instead she had moved out here, after the family doctor warned her she was headed for a nervous breakdown if she did not relieve some of the tension. He felt making a clean break would be a good idea, moving somewhere else where she would not have constant reminders of Gary. Claire had agreed that might be a good idea, although sweet Dr. Beamish thought all her memories were good ones.

Elliot's door slammed, chiming in with hers, and Claire felt the panic building again. *Oh, God,* she found herself praying with desperate haste, *I know I have no right to ask anything of You but please, please . . .* she couldn't even frame the words. What was she asking, anyway? It was too late to speculate further, for Elliot was walking up the buckling sidewalk toward her. His steps were slow, measured, almost as if he were uncertain. It was too dark now to see his face, and Claire waited, hands clasped in front of her, head held high, the house key dangling from one of the tightly clenched fingers.

He stopped a few feet away, then silently held out his own hand, and Claire moved toward him trance-like, then dropped the keys into the outstretched palm. The moon had not yet risen, and would be behind the clouds anyway, and Claire had not left on a light.

"Can you see?" Elliot asked.

"The sidewalk is pretty uneven," Claire warned somewhat breathlessly.

"So is my heartbeat," murmured Elliot.

"Oh!" Without the slightest warning a giggle bubbled its way up her throat and escaped. They climbed the few steps, and Elliot opened the door, flicking on the porch light, then the hall light in the entrance way. They stared at one another in the yellow glow, and the grin continued to tug at her mouth, her heart. She had never met anyone who made her want to laugh like this, and it was a disconcerting, strange feeling.

"Would you . . . would you like to come in for a few minutes?"

Had she really said that? Oh, what had happened to her brain tonight, to have been turned to sawdust simply because this man had coaxed open the closed door of her heart and shown her how good it felt to laugh? He was an architect, for crying out loud. A highly trained, highly paid professional who could only be contemptuous, or even worse, patronizing, toward Claire Gerard, with her B.S.I.D. degree that qualified her only to design single dwellings under a specified number of square feet.

"Your eyes are not your only expressive feature," he said.

Elliot placed her keys on the narrow table just inside the door. He smiled down at her, his ebony hair tousled and his teeth flashing white in the tanned planes of his lean face. Then he added, "No, my shy, scared little kitten, as much as I would love to come in for a few minutes, I'm not going to accept your invitation."

The smile deepened at Claire's undisguised confusion.

"You're not?" she echoed, then raged inwardly for sounding like such a gauche fool.

Of course, though. She had been right all along about him. Why on earth would he want to come in? He was only being polite to follow her home—he had even said so.

"Hmm," murmured Elliot. "They're back to turbulent brown again. Now what is it?"

He pondered a moment, his gaze scanning the narrow entrance hall and beyond, into her office with the framed drawings of houses she had designed just visible. He brought his gaze back to Claire's face, eyes narrowing at her defensive, almost hostile posture.

Finally he said, "Ah, yes. I'm the exalted architect and you're the humble designer whose hesitant invitation was rejected. Am I right?"

Piqued by his perception but admiring nonetheless, Claire gathered her reserve about her like a heavy cloak.

"The invitation was as meaningless as your pretense at regret," she stared him straight in the eye. "I was actually hoping you'd refuse."

"Little shrew." He touched her nose, watched without expression the automatic flinching. "I have to go out of town day after tomorrow—I've been asked to design a new sanctuary and educational complex for a church in San Jose. You won't have to peek around corners, dreading my untimely appearance on

38

your turf, Ms. Gerard.'' He paused, took a step and opened the door. "But you haven't seen the last of me, so start working on accepting that. I have at least as much faith as a mustard seed, and if I can't move a mountain yet I still believe I can move one sweet southern lady to change her mind about me. Good-night, kitten.''

CHAPTER 3

Two weeks crawled by. The third Sunday after Elliot had left Claire started her day as usual, sliding on jeans and a loose knit top and sipping coffee as she watched the sunrise. She had planned to work for a couple of hours and then drive over to the site of the A-frame she had designed for the car salesman. But something nagged at her, teased and worried her brain so that she couldn't concentrate on her plans. When she turned on the radio for diversion she realized what it was. It was Sunday. The radio was playing gospel music, and as clearly as that music Claire could hear Elliot's voice. Sunday, he had said, was a day of rest. He hadn't so much as lifted an eyebrow, but Claire squirmed now as she remembered the glaring contrast of his suit next to her faded jeans. He had obviously come from church that day, only Claire had been too defensive to think of such matters.

Well, she was thinking of them now and sighed as she wandered back into the kitchen to pour another cup of coffee. Elliot didn't act like any man she had ever known, and he didn't even act like . . . well, like most of the Christians she had known back in Georgia. Of course, in a small community like Cherry Creek it was hard to think of people as Christians. They were friends, neighbors . . . the butcher, baker and candlestick maker or whatever. Everyone went to one of the three churches the town supported, and it was a part of life. You went to church on Sunday and then went about your business Monday through Friday. Claire had never questioned it until she married Gary and learned the bitter meaning of the word hypocrisy. He attended services faithfully every week, but he . . . then he . . .

"No," Claire announced aloud in the silent room. "I won't think about it. It doesn't do any good." Maybe she hadn't been the best Christian in the world when she married, but she hadn't been the worst either, in spite of the years of hopeless acknowledgment that she obviously had done something wrong. Why else would God punish her with those nightmare years? And of course she had lived a lie, compounding whatever sins she had committed in her past. She had lived a lie, and then, like an ugly, painful boil, the hatred had grown and spread, drowning out the fear, the shame, and the pain until every breath she drew was infested with the destructive emotion.

With increasing restlessness she padded into the two front rooms that comprised her office. Her work room contained her grandfather's mammoth cherry desk and her drafting table, reminders of her life in Georgia. She wandered around the small room, opening the cream vanilla shades to let the sunshine in, running her finger over the dust-laden top of her plans file cabinet, and then suddenly kneeling to pull out a number of the narrow drawers. In a few moments she was surrounded by drifts of blueprints, the evocative aroma of the drafting paper teasing her nostrils. She had never built any of these houses, all of them designed during those awful years as one

41

measure to keep her sanity. She found herself examining them now, a gleeful imp whispering in her ear that doubtless Elliot would think they were amateurish, impractical; the solar house lacking in technical accuracy, the earth home something you'd see in a bad science fiction movie.

Why had he kept showing interest in the Mackleroy's house? He had said it was different, but Claire had seen homes before that were very similar. She had just modified a few details to suit Reba and Fred Mackleroy, giving them that small front porch recessed to shelter them from the rain, and the bay windows stacked one on top of the other to provide a continuous columnar effect extending to both floors that gave the front of the house its own unique look. Yes, Claire told herself determinedly, it was unique. She did have talent. She was highly qualified, and more than capable of holding her own in the world.

With brisk efficiency she replaced the blueprints, then marched across the entrance hall to the room she used as a reception area. There was a smaller desk in here, a rolltop she had found rummaging through a second-hand furniture store in Carmel. She opened it up and flipped through the appointment book she kept, noting with satisfaction that she had two new potential clients scheduled for this week.

She had also promised to have the rough sketches of a Victorian cottage ready for Mrs. Vancouver by Tuesday. That one was going to be a challenge since the elderly widow had a few ideas that would be difficult to formulate in a blueprint. She wanted, for instance, the kitchen to be a replica of the one she and her husband had in their first home.

". . . and we simply must have the space for the range." Mrs. Vancouver had insisted.

She was a tiny little lady who always wore a hat, lace-edged gloves, and carried an umbrella. Claire also had found out that this supposedly stereotypical character carried a can of mace in her purse and her beloved husband's old hunting knife was strapped on her thigh beneath her petticoat. "World isn't what it used to be," she had affirmed to Claire with a twinkle. "Not that it was that peaceful before. But like I was saying, my dear, Arthur bought the stove the year we married, in 1928, and it works as well now as it did then. You're no laggard, girl, so figure a way to fit it in my box of a kitchen." The stove was a monster of steel and porcelain, a combination gas and woodburning marvel that would require a stovepipe as well as a vent fan. Claire had gently protested, been silenced, and then when she suggested a larger kitchen Mrs. Vancouver had snorted. "Pshaw! With my arthritis and Nellie's grumbling? I did tell you my cousin will be living with me, didn't I?"

"Yes, ma'am." Claire had suppressed a sigh, and finished meticulously jotting down Mrs. Vancouver's specifications.

Well, maybe she should spend today working on the problem of the kitchen, she ruminated now. Hopefully she could immerse herself in work and quit brooding about Elliot Ramsey. He might consider Sunday a day of rest, even worship, but she had more important things to do. Didn't she?

By eleven o'clock she admitted defeat, yanked her sweater off the bentwood coat rack and stormed out. She couldn't concentrate because she felt guilty. Not only did she feel guilty, she felt trapped as well. Trapped, frustrated, depressed . . . she had migrated all the way across the country to escape these feelings, and now they were creeping back again like the infamous kudzu vines back home. If she didn't do something she would be choked, swallowed up, and lose herself completely.

Without conscious thought she climbed into her car and drove off, spending the next hours wandering first south, then north on California's famous seaside

43

Route 1. Midafternoon found her moving inland, and only when she passed the sign announcing the outskirts of Salinas did she at last admit to the secret longing she was about to satisfy. She only had to stop at one gas station to find directions to the new bank designed by Elliot. For long moments she sat inside her car in the parking lot, just staring at it. Of course, banks had all the money in the world so they could afford all those eye-catching luxuries like diagonally laid redwood exterior and round stained glass windows.

Although Claire had tried her hand at some modern designs in college, she had never had the flair for them that Elliot did. Of course, there had not been anyone back within the radius of Cherry Creek who would have been caught dead with a "modern" home, and many a time Claire had stifled the frustration of designing two and three bedroom traditional houses. By the time she had been designing two years, the bulk of her income came from reprints instead of originals. "Why the griping?" Gary had complained on more than one occasion. "You make more money off the reprints anyway, and it sure is easier. Listen, why don't you come on to the party with me? Take a bath in some of that bath oil I gave you for your birthday—ammonia and ink never were my favorite scents, honey-pie."

Neither had alcohol, cigarettes, and cheap after-shave been hers. After awhile there had been cheap perfume mingling with the others in Gary's clothes when he finally came home, but by that time Claire had been relieved instead of incensed.

With almost reckless disregard she pulled back out into the traffic, ignoring the irritated blast of a car's horn as she fled the demons of self-pity and guilt.

The phone was ringing as she was unlocking the door to her house. Dropping purse and keys and sweater in a heap on the narrow occasional table in the foyer, she dashed to answer before it quit ringing. She might not be out begging for customers, but she couldn't afford to miss one, either.

"Dream Designs," she answered with a cool serenity that belied her thumping heart and hurried breathing.

"So, you're finally home. I suppose you've been prowling around a site all afternoon."

"Elliot!" Her heart wasn't thumping now—it was trying to climb out of her rib cage.

"Who else knows all the patterns of your day and the quirks of your personality? How are you doing, my sweet southern belle?"

He might be teasing, but she was not going to respond to the easy warmth, the intimate insinuation that he knew her that well. "I'm doing fine, thank you. And I'm not your sweet southern belle."

Elliot laughed, and the sound blew into her ear like a gentle summer breeze, caressing and tantalizing. "Which one do I have to leave off—being mine, or being sweet? You can't very well deny your roots or your gender."

He wasn't there to see the reluctant smile that lit her face, and Claire was grateful. She was determined to keep from making a fool of herself again. "I'm not yours, and I definitely won't be very sweet if you don't tell me why you're calling."

"Sheathe the claws, kitten." There was a pause before he continued evenly, "I'm calling to let you know I'll be back in town Friday evening, and would like to spend Saturday with you. I thought I'd take you around the Seventeen Mile Drive, and we could have a picnic on the beach. I have another commitment in the evening, but my day is free."

"I don't think it would be a good idea, Elliot," Claire stated, the words dragging out.

"Why am I not surprised to hear that?" was the immediately resigned but still humorous retort.

"Claire . . . we can make this easy or difficult. You might be the perfect example of a human snapping turtle, but I just happen to know where a snapping turtle's soft spots are."

Claire ground her teeth together and clenched her jaw. She would not laugh, and she would not ask. On the other hand . . . "Oh, all right, I'll bite." With a gasp she realized she had fallen into the game, and when Elliot chuckled appreciatively she felt her jaw slackening and her mouth widening again in response. "What soft spots could a snapping turtle possibly have?"

"They're right next to the neck when his head is extended ready to bite the hand that's trying to stroke him." His voice deepened a notch. "What would you do, little snapping turtle, if I closed my hands over your soft spots?"

The verbal picture he painted was so suggestive that for a timeless moment Claire hung suspended in a delicious anticipation she had never experienced before. Then the reality of what he meant permeated her brain, and the picture she imagined now was a nightmare. Grotesque masculine hands were wrapped about her pliant, vulnerable neck, which was extended to the breaking point. Breaking point. The breaking point. She had reached that point once and never planned to again. Never, never again.

"Claire? What is it?"

She hadn't even realized she must have spoken the words aloud, but Elliot's voice came over the phone, the relaxed humor vanished now as he spoke to her sharply. She tried to speak, even opened her mouth, but no words came.

"Claire!" Elliot repeated. "Something's wrong. I can feel it all the way up here in San José. Was it what I said about my hands over your soft spots?"

He was too perceptive, too quick. With a reflex action she would regret for hours, Claire dropped the

46

phone back in the cradle. She could never explain—
she had no desire to even try. It was her burden, her
load of guilt, and she would never dream of sharing it
with anyone. Gary had fooled them all, and because
he had, Claire had had to fool everyone as well. Her
parents, her friends, the minister . . . everyone. She
was not going to blurt out the shameful details of her
life to a man she had only met a month or so ago.
Especially one who placed so much faith and trust in
God. He would either mouth platitudes, or be forced
into the untenable position of agreeing that the God of
wrath and justice had laid His heavy hand upon one
guilty Claire Gerard.

The phone started ringing again, but Claire ignored
it. She walked with unseeing step back out the front
door, and for the next hour strolled the beach. The
tide, the undulation of waves, the endless roar of the
surf were all changeless within their constant change.
The dichotomy of this had provided a soothing escape
for Claire ever since she moved out here. It was an
unction, a balm for her troubled soul and she always
sought it whenever events threatened to overwhelm
her hard-won composure.

The week dragged by as sluggishly as the two
previous ones, although this time Claire was unable to
use the palliative of work. Mrs. Vancouver had been
understanding about the delay, but she had not tried
to hide her disappointment. Claire renewed her
efforts, spending long hours at her drafting table
drawing, erasing, and ultimately discarding. The
kitchen did not want to be designed.

In an effort to distance herself from that project,
Claire spent two entire mornings at the Mackleroy's
house. The electrician was an agreeable young man
who had taken her on as his helper. "Without pay, of
course," he had grinned and winked at her solemnly.
Claire had stapled wires and strung them, and learned
a little more about the trade. The fluffy yellow

insulation was in now, the plastic stapled over it and the construction workers had started dry-walling on the first floor. She spoke to Chuck several times, even tried once again to have the recessed window seats and wider sills included. Chuck has shrugged his massive shoulders. "I'll do anything you want if you can persuade the Mackleroy's to fork over the dough." He had waved her aside with a sweaty hand and disappeared outside to yell at one of the men.

On Thursday Claire once more yielded to the curiosity that had never gone away. The odds were against her ever seeing Elliot Ramsey again, but his shadow was ever present at her shoulder, hovering like the sword of Damocles. It whispered in her ear, telling her that Elliot would have no trouble designing Mrs. Vancouver's kitchen. It dogged her footsteps down the beach, destroying her quest for peace. It insinuated itself into her dreams, and she would wake drenched in sweat from macabre dreams of hands that plundered her body while she lay tied in ropes of wet, green kelp, helpless and screaming soundlessly. So after failing to force down her lunch of grilled cheese sandwich and pear salad on a wilted piece of lettuce, Claire drove to Monterey.

It had been easy to find the address of Elliot's office in the yellow pages. Finding the street was another matter, although Monterey was not that large. She was successful at last, however, and this time parked across the street instead of in the parking lot to the side of the building. As she had anticipated, as she had feared, Elliot's suite of offices was a masterpiece of architectural genius. The building was designed in contemporary lines, but he had used old brick and put in floor-to-ceiling windows normally associated with turn-of-the-century structures. The overall effect was stunning. On the front side, next to the carved wooden doors embellished with beveled glass windows, was a heavy brass plaque.

From her car across the street Claire could just make out the words "Elliot Ramsey, AIA." For many long moments she sat there, unaware of the heat of the bright sunny day, the vaguely curious stares of passers-by, or the stream of traffic flowing past on the street. Eventually she lifted her hand and turned the key. The engine grumbled to life, and Claire drove home.

She was sitting at the table Saturday morning, listlessly crunching a piece of toast and listening to the radio. So lost was she in a jumbled world of confused thoughts that at first the distinctive ding-a-ling of the doorbell did not register. Only when someone pounded on the door did she realize she had company. For no apparent reason she found her mouth was dry, her palms clammy. There was not time to change out of her scruffy faded housecoat, and her hair was a tangled mass of uncombed curls spilling about her head and brushing her shoulders.

"Who is it?" she managed to call through the panels of the door. She knew better than to reveal her state of undress as her reason for not opening it.

"It's Elliot, Claire. Open the door."

"I'm not dressed." The words burst out in haste, and she grimaced at the irony of her loss of common sense.

"So what? I want to talk to you about something."

"No!" she shouted aloud. "I don't want to talk, Elliot."

There was no response to this. Claire listened carefully, but heard nothing. Had he left? She found to her incredulous dismay that she was shocked—and disappointed. Fingers scrambled to unfasten the safety chain as she hastily turned the bolt and yanked open the door. Elliot was standing there, and before she could do more than gasp he had shouldered past and was inside.

"I refuse to engage in a yelling match with a door between us and all the neighbors and morning joggers listening avidly." He swept a comprehensive, amused gaze over her. "Isn't this a little unusual? It's ten o'clock and the fanatically dedicated Claire Gerard is still *á deshabille*, I believe is the euphemistic way of putting it."

Claire wrapped defensive arms about her waist and backed away from him. "Elliot, go away, please. I told you I don't want to talk."

His face softened. "I know you did, honey, and I know I'm being unforgivably aggressive." He took a few steps, making sure he maintained a comfortable distance between them. Claire looked ready to bolt, but he had been desperate himself. The week had been interminable, and he had suffered the agonies of the condemned every time he thought about the stupid, thoughtless words he had teased her with last Sunday. Yet that was not the reason he had come today. He knew better than to confront her with that issue when she was still so wary and untrusting. *Help me out, Lord, will You? I think I might be getting in over my head this time.*

"Look, if you'll let me explain—give me ten minutes—I promise you'll understand. If you still want me to leave then, I will. Okay?"

She shot him a brief, suspicious glare. "You promise?"

He nodded, his face solemn.

"I guess it would be all right, then," she conceded grudgingly. With self-conscious gestures she ran her hands through her hair, down the front of her housecoat. "I—it's just that you caught me off guard. I wasn't expecting anyone this morning, and nobody ever calls this early on weekends." With determined grace she straightened up, dropped the defensive posture. "If you'll give me five minutes I'll go and dress. You can wait in there." She indicated the room behind him she used as her reception area.

"Sure," Elliot agreed with an easy smile. He turned and wandered into the room, looking around with interest as he heard Claire move swiftly away. He knew she was disconcerted by his unexpected appearance, and was regretful. Yet if he had phoned first he most likely would have been treated to the same response he had been given Sunday night. Claire Gerard was definitely an enigma. He pondered the imitation oriental carpet that covered the floor, the serviceable chairs scattered about the small room. There might not be an abundance of wealth indicated, but Claire was nonetheless a classy lady who knew how to arrange what she had for best effect. He strolled over to the rolltop desk, bending down for a closer look. This was a nice piece, and original, if he was not badly mistaken. Whoever had refinished it had done a nice job.

"What are you doing?"

He rose leisurely, squashing the inward pang at the note of hostility in her voice. "I'm admiring your desk. Did you find it here, or did it once belong to a favorite great-uncle back in Georgia?"

Some of the hostility faded. "I found it here." She sat down in one of the chairs, indicating that she was ready to end the idle chitchat. "All right. I'm dressed. What do you want, Elliot?"

He obediently sat down in a chair across from her, the gray-blue eyes surveying her jeans and blouse, the hastily combed hair and face without make-up. She was too tense still, with her feet stiffly resting flat on the floor, her hands nervously stroking the chair arms, her face blank as an empty television screen.

"I want to tell you about Nature's Journeymen," he began slowly, watching with satisfaction the array of expressions that flitted across her countenance.

"Nature's Journeymen?" Claire repeated. What was he talking about? Why wasn't he bringing up her behavior of a week ago?

51

Elliot stretched out his own jean-clad legs and contemplated his beat-up cowboy boots briefly before lifting his gaze to Claire. He smiled. "Nature's Journeymen is an organization I founded five years ago. It's for backpackers and is sort of like the Sierra Club only on a much lesser scale." His smile broadened to a grin as he watched Claire struggle— and fail—to hide her bewilderment. "The treks only take place in the summer months, mainly because I'm too busy to take off more time." He leaned back in the pub chair, resting his head against the worn fabric back and closing his eyes. "Sometimes I have a hard time convincing myself to keep it that way. When I'm up in the mountains it's a strong temptation to chuck my architectural career and try to make a go of Nature's Journeymen year-round."

Claire stared at him, lying slouched, as relaxed and boneless as a rag doll, as at home as if he did this all the time. "Where did you come up with the name?" she asked hurriedly, ordering her mind to cease such forbidden speculations.

Elliot laughed, sat up and dangled his hands between his knees as he answered. "You might find this hard to believe, but it came from *Hamlet*."

"Shakespeare? You founded a backpacking organization named after a Shakespearean tragedy?"

"Has a good ring to it, doesn't it? I believe it, too, Claire, about being journeymen of nature. Do you understand the context, in the medieval sense, of the word 'journeyman'? It's a man—" he stopped, grinned wider, "—only nowadays it's men and women—who has fully served his apprenticeship in whatever the trade was, and is considered to be a fully qualified worker for his employer."

Thoroughly bemused, Claire could only murmur, "First an architect, then a nature nut, now a scholar. What other caps do you wear, Mr. Ramsey?"

"The eloquent advocate cap, perhaps? I'm hoping

to paint such an enticing picture of Nature's Journeymen that it will be easy to persuade you to sign up for one of the treks this summer.''

"What?'' Claire could only blink rounded eyes at him, so disconcerted by the entire conversation that she was stymied for any other verbal reply.

"I can tell you're impressed,'' Elliot intoned dryly. He stood up with a sudden swift grace that looked effortless, and moved over to Claire. "Come to the window with me for a minute,'' he ordered, holding out his hand.

Claire started to put hers out, realized what she was doing and snatched it back. Rising, she edged around his lean but nonetheless imposing body and walked over to the windows.

Elliot joined her, once again allowing her at least three feet of space between them. "What do you see?'' he asked, his voice quiet, encouraging.

"The street . . . houses,'' Claire responded, turning a questioning face to him. "And the ocean beyond, of course. That's why I leased this house.''

"Can you imagine what it would look like if you looked out and saw nothing but palms, a few scrub oaks, the beach, and then nothing but an endless expanse of water?''

"Well, I suppose. Elliot, what are you trying to say?'' A thread of impatience laced the words and she saw his mouth dent.

"I'm trying to help you begin to understand the purpose of Nature's Journeymen. Claire, when God made man He also gave him dominion over the earth. I happen to believe that we've made a pretty fair mess of things, mainly because we've never tried to work at training ourselves properly to take care of what we were given. The organization I formed has a two-fold purpose. One is to teach people how to literally be nature's journeymen: see for themselves the beauty and wonder of God's creation where it has been

53

largely untouched by man's hand." He gestured to the outside view. "Around here all you can enjoy is bits and pieces, all of it marred by our insatiable desire to grab our own little kingdom, and if we can't grab it we can make money at the ultimate expense of nature. My organization was created to try and instill in the participants a knowledge of the nature God put into our care." He drew a deep breath and his voice dropped to almost a crooning whisper. "When you're up in the mountains, and all the streets, houses and cars are gone, you're left with nothing but surroundings that have been around since the dawn of creation. Claire, it's so easy to feel the presence of God up there. And then it's only a short step to all the ways we can help restore, renew, and protect the natural resources we have left."

He looked down at her, and a faint band of red stained the strong, tanned cheekbones. "I sound like a man on a soapbox, don't I?"

"A little," Claire admitted, but her eyes were full of what he had said. "It sounds wonderful, though."

She looked back out the window again, this time with a rapt, dreamy expression on her face as she allowed her imagination to take hold. When Elliot's hand fell softly onto her shoulder she barely flinched, so caught up in the spell was she.

"Let's go for that drive," Elliot coaxed, moving infinitesimally closer when she didn't jerk immediately free of his hand. "We can eat on the beach, like I promised, and you'll understand even better."

Eyes as clear and green as a new spring leaf lifted to gaze up into his face, and Elliot felt a queer spasm swell in his midsection. Then the spasm tautened until it hurt as he watched awareness flood her eyes, turbulent muddy brown drowning out the green.

"Claire," he murmured in protest, "don't look at me like that."

Claire walked over behind her desk, flipped through

her appointment book with hands that did not even know what they were doing. "Like what?" she inquired, her voice cool, brittle.

Elliot stayed by the window, clasping his hands behind his back as he watched the woman on the other side of the room.

"It's hard to describe, actually," he began slowly, carefully.

He paused, bowed his head as if lost in thought, then his attitude and voice changed to brisk determination. "Tell you what. I'll come up with a way to describe it while we drive down to Pebble Beach, okay? Then we can both share lunch as well as our thoughts."

It was tempting, so very tempting. She had not dated at all since Gary's death two years ago; she had not wanted to date. She still had no desire to pursue any kind of relationship with a man, and yet she was drawn to Elliot Ramsey in a way that was short-circuiting all the programs she had formulated in her brain.

"You'll tell me more about Nature's Journeymen?" she asked now, reluctant to let him see the curiosity he had aroused but unable to withhold the question. Maybe if he thought her only reason for going was to find out about his backpacking club and perhaps agree to sign up for the June trek, he would not see through to the other reason.

Claire was still almost too frightened to admit it to herself, but a few minutes ago, when his hand had rested so gently upon her shoulder and hadn't bothered her, she had to face the main reason she wanted to go. She was attracted to Elliot, and trying to deny those feelings only increased their intensity.

She was like a cautious bug drawn to the fascinating but deadly Venus fly-trap. Only this time, Claire mused dismally, the bug might very well poison the plant first. What would the dedicated, caring Elliot

Ramsey do if he ever found out that the woman he was pursuing had prayed daily that her husband would disappear from her life forever? That when he *had* died she had shed tears of relief, not sorrow?

CHAPTER 4

IT WAS A WARM, periwinkle-blue-sky day. Elliot drove slowly, and with the windows down and the wind teasing and tantalizing, Claire gradually found herself relaxing. She still wasn't sure exactly how Elliot had maneuvered her out of the house and into his car, but she decided to just let go and ride with the tide for this one brief moment.

"Pretty confident of me, weren't you?" she commented in a neutral tone, her solemn eyes watching him without expression. They were also an ambiguous shade that was neither green nor brown, which could either have revealed a lot—or nothing at all.

Elliot glanced across at her. "I'm never confident where you're concerned," he intoned with dry deprecation, his mouth widening in a smile when Claire's eyebrows lifted. "So why don't you tell me exactly what it is that I'm so confident of?"

"That I would come with you." Her eyes fell to his hands, resting with easy strength on the steering wheel. A sliver of raw feeling, frightening in its intensity, suddenly shot through her, and she hastily averted her gaze. "I saw the picnic basket in the trunk when you tossed my windbreaker back there. What would you have done if I had refused?"

"Eaten in solitary splendor." His smile broadened as he turned off the road and into the entrance of the Seventeen-Mile Drive. After stopping briefly at the small stone building that housed an elderly guard and showing him some sort of identification card, they made their way down the winding lane. Some of the wealthiest people on the West Coast owned homes on this tiny peninsula, and Claire gazed in mute astonishment at the overt display of material possessions. The drive was lined with trees and wound its way in serpentine curves among all the palatial residences. Most of them were protected either by high walls or an abundance of careful landscaping, but Claire was still able to enjoy them, including a number of smaller homes that were nonetheless leagues above her own economic status.

"I'd love to design a home like some of these," she whispered beneath her breath, catching it as they passed one particularly splendid example of what unlimited amounts of money could achieve.

Elliot shot her a cool, assessing gaze. "You never know what the future holds." He kept half an eye on her as they abruptly came out of the shadows and drove into blinding sunlight. On one side the manicured perfection of the Pebble Beach golf course lay like an emerald green carpet, while to the other the Pacific Ocean stretched into infinity. "Do you have a lot of dreams, Claire?"

Claire was gazing raptly out the window at the view. "What?" she asked absently, and Elliot chuckled.

Pulling into a parking area, he switched off the ignition and turned toward Claire. "Would you like to get out?" he asked, eyes twinkling at her barely restrained eagerness. She acted like she had never

58

been here before, yet he knew she had lived in the area for over a year now. What did she do in her spare time? Did she allow herself any? He followed her as she moved with her usual restrained grace across the parking lot, his curiosity growing by leaps and bounds.

There were other people scattered about, but they faded to insignificant specks in a canvas where sea and sky met and blended in shades of luminous blue-green. Large boulders, rolled and tumbled and then flung haphazardly to shore, formed an irresistible lure beckoning Claire's feet. Huge strands of kelp with tentacles as thick as her wrist draped across the rocks with almost macabre seductiveness, then trailed off and disappeared in the foaming surf. She didn't even notice Elliot joining her, for her eyes were riveted to the kelp and her mind was riveted by the memory of her awful nightmares.

He studied her for a moment in silence. "I would have thought you'd been here a number of times by now," he ventured at last, his voice casual.

"Not here," Claire answered. "I've driven by the entrance before but never took the time." Her eyes could not leave the kelp, and suddenly she shuddered. "It's incredible," she found herself repeating the thought aloud as if propelled by some inner force.

"Why do I get the feeling you're not talking about the beauty of sea and sky?" Elliot murmured, his eyes narrowing as they followed the direction of Claire's unswerving gaze. "What is so incredible, Claire?" he repeated gently, hand lifting and just brushed the soft curve of her cheek.

"The—the kelp," Claire stammered, moving back a step in spite of the fact that her gaze was riveted now on Elliot. She felt as if he were a powerful magnet, able to pull free all her feelings, all her secrets as if they were no more than minuscule iron shavings helpless in the face of an overwhelming force. "It's exactly like my dream."

"What dream is that?"

His voice was low, his stance totally nonthreatening, yet Claire suddenly froze, her defenses snapping back into place. "It's nothing," she said with a shrug. "The kelp is fascinating, isn't it? Sort of like those giant sea monsters from *20,000 Leagues Under the Sea*, or a creature out of a Star Wars movie."

"I'm more fascinated by your dream," Elliot replied, eyes flashing with determined silver. "If you'll remember I already asked if you had any, but the way you looked just now was more like you were remembering a nightmare instead of a dream. Talk to me, Claire. Open yourself up for a change. I really want to know."

She wanted to share, with a need that went beyond the rational. He was so strong, so kind, and he acted sincere. He had subtly but thoroughly insinuated himself into her life and Claire, for the first time in years, found herself tempted to reveal part of herself.

"You can't want to know," she blurted, because at the same time she had acknowledged her need to share she had also realized what would have to be revealed.

With a courtly gesture Elliot indicated she should walk back toward the car; he had not touched her again, however, and as Claire began picking her way across the rocks to the parking lot she wondered just exactly how much this man saw with those oh, so clear eyes of his.

"Why don't you let me be the judge of that?" he said in a quiet voice as they walked. At the car he lifted out the picnic basket and then led Claire to a fairly private strip of sand on the narrow beach where visitors were allowed. After spreading a faded blanket, he and Claire laid out the meal. As he poured her soft drink into a paper cup he glanced across to where she sat.

"Talk to me now, Claire. Tell me the reason for the

shadows that fill those lovely eyes sometimes. What nightmares are haunting you, hmm?"

Claire bit into her sandwich, a thick, creamy chicken salad delight. She lifted surprised eyes to Elliot as she chewed. He grinned but did not speak. "I dream I'm tied up in ropes of kelp," she finally dragged out, her voice slow, halting. She couldn't look at Elliot and kept her eyes fastened on the delicious sandwich in her hand. "I can't get free and I keep trying to scream but I can't." She stopped, pressing her lips together to keep from blurting out the worst part. With a determined air of brightness she lifted her head. "Sounds sort of silly and melodramatic in the daytime, doesn't it?"

"Sounds frightening," Elliot refuted with extreme gentleness. "No wonder you were staring at the kelp as if it were about to reach up and grab you."

Claire lifted restless shoulders. "Well, I've told you now. It's just a stupid dream, and I have enough on my mind without dwelling on silly nightmares. Tell me more about Nature's Journeymen."

"In a moment." He finished off his drink, then lay back on the blanket, propped on his elbows as his gaze moved over Claire in the probing inventory. "Something happened to you before you moved out here, didn't it? You put on a good show—a cool, poised lady with a career on the rise and her act all together. Only it is an act, isn't it? Somewhere inside the sophisticated woman of the world is a scared little girl crying out for help."

"Don't you think you're being a bit glib, a bit pat with your analysis, Mr. Ramsey?"

His gaze took in her turbulent eyes, her mouth. "Am I?"

She turned away from him and sat, arms about her drawn up knees as she looked out over the ocean. Nearby a family with two children was talking and laughing. Seagulls called and dived into the water, and the sound of the surf and the wind rolled over and around her. "I don't know. I'm not used to talking about myself, Elliot. It's easier not to. Can we talk about your organization instead? It's far more interesting and—"

"Relax, Claire."

She heard him shift, felt his presence behind her and stiffened. He mustn't come too close. He mustn't, or she would panic. She felt it building inside, fighting and scrabbling like maniacal demons to overpower her will and transform her into the weak, trembling and finally hateful creature she used to be.

"I told you there was a two-fold purpose for Nature's Journeymen." He had moved to sit beside her, that was all. He wasn't going to make a pass, or touch her in any way. Claire slowly turned her head and met the rich compassion of his gaze. "Learning to appreciate and take care of nature was one. But the other one is learning to appreciate and come to know yourself, and if you're a Christian, developing a deeper relationship with our Lord." His eyes burned with a silver fire that seared her helplessly entrapped senses. "I've met a lot of people, led hundreds of them on treks, but never have I met anyone who needs Nature's Journeymen more than you, Claire Gerard. We're having a meeting on Tuesday night at seven-thirty. I want you to come."

Mrs. Vancouver's kitchen had finally allowed itself to be designed. Claire sat hunched over her drawing table, allowing herself a brief inward pat for her ingenious solution. Even Elliot Ramsey couldn't have done any better. She straightened with a groan, pressing the small of her back with her hands as she loosened up some of the kinks incurred over the last six hours. All she had left to do now was the markings indicating placement of lighting fixtures, and then she could start on the Davis home. Of course, first she needed to call Mrs. Vancouver with the good news, and there were two potential clients whose calls she had yet to return. She hadn't been out to the Mackleroy's house, either, much less the site of the salesman's house where the foundation had just been poured.

Groaning again, Claire flicked off the lamp and slid off the stool, wandering over to the window and gazing outside. It was late afternoon, and a mellow spring sun was bathing the world in shades of gold and amber. She could just catch the dancing light gleaming off the ocean's restless surface, and she wondered if a walk down the beach was in order. The last several days it hadn't seemed to help, for she was still restless and tense, still subconsciously waiting to hear from Elliot. It was Thursday now, and she had heard nothing—not a word.

After wrestling with her conscience like Jacob with the angel, Claire had decided to participate in the trek. Elliot had neither gloated nor shown elation, although he very easily could have exhibited both. Claire appreciated his forbearance, but she was still unnerved by his uncanny ability to cut straight through to the heart.

"You need something, Claire," he had told her. "I think you need God, but I am not going to force my faith on you. But, Claire," he had hesitated, gazing at her with such intensity that Claire had shrunk back. Elliot had winced before he finished what he had to say. "Claire, if you would give God a chance, He might surprise you. Just as I have, remember? Think about it, and come to the meeting Tuesday."

Well, she had gone to the meeting at a conference room in a Monterey motel, and she had been suitably impressed by the organization, as well as the wide spectrum of people who participated in Nature's Journeymen. The room had been packed, and she had noted everything from crisp business suits to rumpled jeans and sweatshirts. Giggling teenagers sat next to sober middle-aged executives, and the aura of excitement and enthusiasm was contagious. By the evening's end Claire was officially signed up for Nature's Journeymen Trek IIB, and her first meeting with the nine other members of that trek had been scheduled.

She had not had a single opportunity, however, to speak with Elliot. He had smiled over at her once while she was standing in a line waiting to have her trek time confirmed. The lissome, leggy blonde behind the table had said, "Oh, you're Claire Gerard," and handed her a bulky envelope. "Elliot said to tell you these all need to be filled out as soon as possible. It's all the data forms for a physical. It's self-explanatory, but call if you have any questions. I'm Rhonda, by the way, Elliot's secretary and general dogsbody for Nature's Journeymen."

Claire had gazed in bemusement at the thick envelope, and when her head lifted, her eyes met Elliot's. He had smiled that bone-softening smile at her and then winked. Claire had blushed, thanked Rhonda, and moved aside, secretly hoping he would find a chance to speak to her.

He hadn't, of course. It had been stupid and silly to hope, for there had been over a hundred people packed into the room and Elliot had far more pressing matters to take care of than to indulge in light conversation with a starstruck woman who should know better by now. But though her mind might know better, her heart had hoped for more.

And now it was Thursday, and he still hadn't chosen to get in touch with her. She toyed with the pull on the shades, then turned and stalked across the hall to her desk to find the names of those two clients. If he wanted to be that way, so be it. She would not sit here pining by the phone. She had better things to do.

The Davis house was not going well. Mr. Davis was an avid gardener, and wanted an atrium incorporated into the living room area. It was Friday now, and almost eight o'clock at night. Claire had been working on the rough draft since morning, and her eyes were gritty, stinging from the intense concentration. Her back was on fire, and her neck felt as if gigantic jaws were crunching into it. She had taken time for a quick sandwich around noon, but had not stirred from the stool since, and her frustration now bordered on tears and desperation. Never had she had such a hard time concentrating, and never had designing been such a herculean struggle. She had even taken the phone off the hook, for the few times it had rung it had completely destroyed her tenuous train of thought. At the rate she was going she wouldn't have to worry about clients anyway. She would have to close up shop and do something that didn't require a brain—because at the moment she wondered whether or not she had one.

The doorbell rang.

"Peter Piper picked a peck of pickled peppers!" she snapped aloud. Mom had always used tongue-twisters to vent frustration, and Claire had adopted the habit. It was better than swearing, her mother always said, and usually served to break the tension as well. This time it didn't work.

Claire slammed down her pencil. She stood up but had to grab the stool as the room swayed around her. While she coped with vertigo and numb legs the doorbell rang again, followed by heavy knocking.

Claire staggered across the office and flung open the door, prepared to give short shrift to the paperboy or salesman or—or Elliot Ramsey? With a strangled gasp of disbelief she sagged against the portal. Of all the times . . .

"You look terrible," he observed frankly. "Claire, are you ill? Why didn't you call me? What's wrong?"

He stepped inside and would have taken her arm, but Claire forced herself to straighten and back away.

"I'm just tired," she said, disarmed by the quick show of concern. She waved in the general direction of her drafting table, exhaustion and surprise loosening her reserve. "I have this house that doesn't want to be designed." She stopped, slanted him a reproachful look. "And it's all your fault, Elliot Ramsey."

She swayed suddenly, lightheaded and dizzy. Elliot's arm shot out to steady her, and before she could spit a retort he was guiding her into the reception area and seating her carefully on the loveseat next to the far wall.

"When was the last time you ate something?"

He was still holding her hands, and Claire pulled them free, relieved when Elliot did not say anything. "I had a sandwich around eleven, I think," she answered with stilted dignity. "I've been busy."

"Too busy to take a fifteen minute break to eat something decent? Too busy to make a trip out to either of the sites you've got going? Too busy to be interrupted by the phone?" He rose from where he had been kneeling beside her and walked over to the phone to place the receiver back in its cradle. Then he returned to Claire and dropped onto the seat beside her. He watched her through half-slitted eyes, but he didn't move.

"I can see I'm going to have to take you in hand to get you in decent shape to go on a trek the end of June," he finally observed, and Claire lifted her shoulders in a shrug.

"I figured you'd forgotten about it," she mumbled.

"Now why would I do that after risking my reputation and the continuation of our relationship to set you up for one?" Elliot inquired, his voice teasing.

Claire sneaked a quick glance up into the silvery blue pools of his eyes. His mouth was smiling, she thought irrelevantly, but his eyes were serious. "I haven't heard from you all week," she found herself complaining, and something twisted her stomach besides hunger pains at the indulgent, knowing look that flashed across his lean features. She added in a peevish rush, "But as you can see I haven't been pining away by the phone. In fact, I think I've changed my mind about going. I have too many other irons in the fire to take the time to go gallivanting around the woods and meet Smokey the Bear."

"Ah, Claire . . ." he leaned back and laughed, the sound of it curling Claire's toes. "What am I going to do with you?" He sat up abruptly, leaning toward her with a look on his face she had never seen, and her heart gave a gigantic leap.

"I know what I want to do, but I'm afraid of what will happen if I try." His voice dropped to a rasping whisper, and one long arm crept down the sofa back behind her head and shoulders. "How long has it been since a man kissed you, Claire?"

Hot color flooded her cheeks, then receded to leave her pale and bleached as driftwood. "Not long enough," she managed to retort, her voice high-pitched and much too thin. She lurched to her feet and then stood there, swaying slightly, as her stampeding senses registered the pain lacerating Elliot's face.

"Elliot?" she questioned hesitantly, almost fearfully.

He jerked forward, worrying his hair with his hands as he kept his face down, away from Claire's stunned perusal. "I'm sorry," he said softly. "That's about the dumbest thing I've said since I was a kid in college."

Claire stared down at the top of his head, and in spite of her galloping pulses felt a smile tug her lips. "I doubt if you were still a kid by the time you were in college," she murmured.

She didn't stop to wonder why she was concerned about sparing Elliot's feelings. She just knew she couldn't stand his pain, his obvious remorse, that she had to try to explain, to reassure.

"Elliot . . . it's me, not you," she struggled for words, forcing herself not to retreat when his head lifted and their eyes met. "Please don't berate yourself. It's just that I don't like to be touched, like you said before," she rushed on, blundering through the explanation. "I realize you don't understand, and I'm sorry, but it's so complicated I don't really know how to tell you."

Her voice faded, then rallied at his encouraging look and sympathetic silence. "You were right about my having been through a bad experience. I guess it's scarred me." She took a deep breath. "I don't talk about it—I can't—but I don't want you to blame yourself for saying what you did. I don't imagine any of the other women you—you kiss ever objected." She gasped as the last impulsive words left her lips, color swarming back in a red tide when Elliot's eyebrows lifted and a chuckle escaped.

"I'm glad you have such a high opinion of my skills." He stood slowly, carefully, as if not to frighten her further. "Claire . . ." his voice went very soft, almost stroking her with tenderness, "thank you for sharing part of your pain with me. I just wish you felt free to share it all." He hesitated, once again lowering his eyes as if in prayer. Claire waited without moving, watching him with the stillness of a butterfly about to flit away from the net.

"Will you answer me one question?" he asked when he lifted his head again, and Claire inclined her head, waiting. "The person who hurt you so badly— will you tell me who it was?"

It had to come, and Claire was almost surprised at the ease with which the words left her lips. "My husband." She was not prepared for Elliot's reaction and stepped back when all the color left his face and his eyes went completely blank.

"You're married?" he choked out in a tortured rasp.

Claire closed her eyes now, the memories sweeping back over her as she was at last forced to say aloud the words she had not had to say since she moved out here. She had made sure no one had the opportunity to ask—until Elliot Ramsey. "He's dead. I'm a widow."

Elliot's tense shoulders slumped, and he murmured, "Thank God," with such heartfelt relief that it was a minute before the implications hit either of them. A faint band of red stained Elliot's cheeks now, and he lifted his hand in apology.

"I didn't mean it that way," he began awkwardly. Claire was staring at him strangely, her eyes so wide they filled her face. He watched as she opened her mouth to speak but no words came out and he told himself he was the biggest, most insensitive fool on earth. *Forgive me, Lord. I got carried away and didn't listen. Will You help me make amends?*

"I'm sorry your husband is dead," he continued evenly, but was stopped again, this time by Claire's violently shaking head.

"Don't say anymore," she begged in a tremulous whisper. "Just—don't say anymore."

He saw she was near breaking, and knew that once again he had to retreat. Patience, however, had always been one of his strong suits, even when he was a boy. He could sit all afternoon waiting for a fish to bite, not stirring a muscle. His father would give up in disgust and roll over and go to sleep, and Elliot would invariably wake him up by flapping the wet fish in his face. Claire Gerard was a fish of a different caliber all together, but she was definitely worth the wait.

"Why don't we have something to eat?" he suggested, deliberately making his voice casual, off-hand. "If you don't feel up to going out, I could order a pizza, or you could yield your kitchen to me and I'll cook supper. You like my chicken salad sandwiches pretty well, as I recall.''

He refused to listen to any of her feeble arguments, gently and persuasively knocking them aside like so many children's building blocks. Claire found herself sitting at her little kitchen table for two watching as he fried up bacon and eggs with all the skill of a short order cook. He watched her like a hawk while she ate, sipping hot chocolate and making conversation about his week. He hadn't come any earlier because he had been in San Jose. There had been a problem with the church he was building. He had in fact just returned to Monterey this evening, and had barely thrown his dirty clothes down before hurrying to Pacific Grove.

"You said you were having a problem with one of your designs,'' he ventured casually as Claire helped him clear the table and put the dishes in the sink. "Since you also said it was my fault, would you condescend to let me look at it? Maybe I could help even if I'm pretty rusty in the home-designing department.''

He waited without taking a breath, acknowledging with heavy bleakness that he was doubtless provoking another cool putdown and hasty retreat. But he was desperate to find a reason to prolong the evening with her, and just as desperate to find some way to keep his wayward mind off its stubbornly physical bent.

The irrational surge of relief that went thundering through her caused Claire to sag against the sink. Was she so weak-spirited, so lacking in professional pride now that she could grasp at whatever alms Elliot cared to dole out? For all his self-effacing remarks he would probably solve the problem in two minutes, leaving Claire drowning in a sea of inadequacy. He had already shaken her foundation until it crumbled; allowing him access to her work would be tantamount to professional suicide. Yet she was so tired. Even after eating Elliot's simple but delicious supper she found it difficult to hold a plate as she rinsed it off in the sink.

"Elliot . . ." she sighed his name helplessly, keeping her back to him so she didn't have to see his face, "I know I ought to, but I can't." She paused, then confessed with painful honesty, "If I let you help I'd never be able to live with myself, knowing I was inadequate and lacking in my career."

He moved behind her and placed his arms on either side of the sink, trapping her there. "Easy," he crooned in her ear as she stiffened and then froze. "Be easy, little one, and let me hold you. You're reeling with exhaustion, Claire. Let me share my strength—I'm not going to hurt you." He kept murmuring soft words as he slowly, gradually brought his arms up and let his hands clasp her forearms. She was quivering like aspen leaves in a high wind, but he closed his mind to her fear. She had to become used to his touch, not only because he needed her to, but because of what she would have to face on the trek.

"Elliot," she gasped, all her senses rioting.

"Shh," he whispered. "Relax. Lean against me, there's a good girl, easy now. That's it." He ran his hands up and down her arms in slow, comforting strokes, forcing his own body to stay relaxed and nonthreatening. "Claire, there's a passage in the book of Matthew where Christ is saying pretty much the same thing. 'Come to me, all you who are weary and burdened, and I will give you rest,' He promised. It's not a sin to reach out for help, Claire, even when it's being offered by a mere man like me." He turned her around, keeping his grip gentle but firm, and looked deeply into her eyes.

"Claire, I care about you. I'm not offering to help out of a feeling of superiority or to make you feel inadequate. I'm here simply as a friend—and my offer of help was in that capacity. Do you understand the difference?"

71

"It's hard to understand anything when you're holding me so close," Claire confessed, her entire body rigid with it warring desires. Part of her wanted to scream and flail, but a large part—an electrifyingly large part—wanted to melt against Elliot.

He smiled, a melting, sweet smile that showered her in its warmth. If he was feeling triumphant he was keeping it carefully concealed. "Show me the plan, my weary little home designer," he wrapped an arm about her shoulders and urged her toward the door that separated her living quarters from the office area.

Claire allowed herself to be led. In truth she could not have prevented it, for she was awash now in a sea of sensation caused by Elliot's closeness. Never had the touch of any man affected her so, not even Gary in those first euphoric, innocent weeks after they met. Claire was not a demonstrative person. Her parents loved her, and told her so through words and actions—but seldom through physical touch. An only child born late in their lives, neither parent felt comfortable showering her with hugs and kisses. Claire grew into a reserved child, and a warm but reserved teenager. There seemed to be a "do not touch" sign posted, and although she dated, the boys seldom came back. Claire knew she had a reputation for being frigid, an ice queen, but it had never bothered her because she had never enjoyed being pawed and panted over anyway.

Gary had been almost twenty years older, and Claire had been a delicious challenge. He had managed to tap the sleeping passions buried so deeply, confusing Claire enough to talk her into marrying him. Her awakening had been brutally shocking, and she had withdrawn into herself so completely she had convinced herself that her lack of desire for the opposite sex was a reality. Ten years had done nothing to convince her otherwise—until tonight.

Was Elliot like Gary? Everything in her shied away

from comparing, but how was he different? He had promised he wouldn't hurt her—Gary had never made a promise like that. He said he cared about her—Gary had bombarded her with declarations of love and passion that ended up meaning nothing. And what about Elliot's deep faith? Surely that ought to make a difference, for the only time Gary had acted devout was Sunday mornings.

What was that verse Elliot had mentioned? As they stopped in front of Claire's drafting table she opened her mouth to ask him, and then remembered she had no right to claim any of the comforts promised by the Son of God. She was unaware of the despair that filled her face, but Elliot was not. She watched the muscles of his jaw flex, his eyes turn to steely gray, and a very different question popped out before she could stop it.

"Why are you looking like that?" she asked, her voice panicked. Had he looked down, seen the partial design, and was it so awful he didn't know what to say? Was he regretting his offer? Had her coldness finally so repulsed him he wanted nothing more to do with her? This last thought was so depressing she almost cried out, for she had come face to face with the knowledge that she very much wanted Elliot Ramsey to keep having something to do with her.

"Like what?" Elliot asked then, his gaze searching her face as his hand lifted and his fingers brushed the corner of her eye.

"Claire . . . are you so afraid of me that it causes you to cry?" His own question was wracked with anguish, and for a long moment they stared at one another, each fighting private battles the other could not yet comprehend.

CHAPTER 5

"I DON'T WANT TO BE afraid of you," Claire finally choked out, the admission sending her lashes down so she wouldn't have to see Elliot's reaction. "And I'm not crying."

"Then praise the Lord and pass the blueprint," Elliot paraphrased, his voice lightening miraculously into relieved laughter. Claire's head snapped up with a jerk. He looked down at her tenderly, and then his hands were cupping her face.

"Do you realize this is the most I've touched you since we met," he breathed with a grin splintering across his face, "and you have yet to scratch and spit and pull away? Show me your plans, my almost purring kitten, and distract me before it goes to my head."

Releasing her, he turned to the drafting table and switched on the lamp. "Is this it?" When Claire nodded he sat down on the stool, one arm drawing her close as he lost himself in the rough draft spread before him. "Client change his mind about this room? What does he want here?"

There was nothing in his voice but interest and enthusiasm, and with a fluttery sigh Claire picked up a pencil. "He's a compulsive gardener, and saw a magazine somewhere with a house that had an atrium as the focal point of the living area. He wants it incorporated into his own home, but he also wants to maintain the eighteen hundred square feet and the same general facade . . . here."

She rummaged beneath the rough draft and produced a sketch of the exterior of the house. Her fingers were unsteady, and Elliot's closed over them briefly.

"Take it easy, love. Everybody needs outside help once in awhile. It's no disgrace, believe me."

"I bet you don't have to."

"Then you'd lose your bet. In fact, I spent a large part of the week conferring with a friend of mine who has offices in San Francisco. I'm not conceited enough to pretend I know all the answers." He released her fingers after giving them a gentle squeeze. "Pride goes before destruction, remember? Now, quit distracting me so I can study this."

"I realize it's probably ridiculously elementary to you," Claire started to apologize, "but I'm afraid I—"

"Will you stow it already?" His easy grin reassured her, and Claire lapsed into silence and watched Elliot. He bent over the plan, idly toying with her pencil as he mulled over the problem. "This is good work," he commented half under his breath, and Claire felt a shaft of liquid pleasure spurt through her. "Neat lettering, too . . . why won't he just let you add a couple of hundred square feet? That shouldn't add but five or six thousand dollars . . ."

Claire looked down at him wryly. "Elliot, this is a middle-class single dwelling, not a multi-million dollar church or office complex. To most people—me included—five or six thousand is a lot of money and

75

most people can't afford that kind of extra bucks." She picked up a scrap piece of sketching paper. "I thought I could do it by knocking out this wall and then having the atrium be one entire side of the living room wall, but I couldn't figure out the wiring or support . . ."

"Wait a minute!" He took the sketch and drew rapidly. "That's no problem. Look, all you have to do is this—"

For the next hour they worked with a harmony Claire never would have believed possible. The builders she had worked with in the past had treated her with indulgence, like a precocious little girl dabbling with a new hobby. Along with the majority of other professional home designers, she had always been wary of close contact with architects. But Elliot was treating her as an equal. He had even complimented her ability, and when he finally decreed her problem solved and stood up, she gazed up at him with her feelings shining out like a neon sign.

Elliot caught his breath, then, moving as if he were underwater, he shoved the stool out of the way and his arms lifted. Claire stood transfixed as he enclosed her in a careful embrace, but she didn't push him away.

"Claire," he murmured above her head as he drew her against his chest, "I think I'm going to kiss you goodnight this time. Do you think you can keep from bolting or snapping my head off?"

There was nothing like a little bit of humor to relax your guard, Claire observed fuzzily as she watched his head lower until his lips were only inches away. He was so strong, yet so gentle, so frightening, yet so safe. Her lids were too heavy to stay open, and as they drooped an acquiescent sigh floated past her throat and out into the stillness of the night.

She felt the warmth and softness of Elliot's mouth brushing hers in a caress so tender tears pricked her eyelids. The gentle pressure lifted, then returned one last time in an almost reverent salute. Claire opened her eyes, blinking away the moisture as Elliot lifted his finger to trace the lips he had just so briefly kissed.

"You're a very sweet and tempting package, Claire Gerard," he held her a little ways from him, smiling at her dazed expression. "You're also a lady with a tremendous amount of talent. Don't underrate it—or yourself—ever again."

"I won't." She returned his smile, her own tremulous, wondering. "Elliot . . . thank you."

He let her go and took a step toward the hall. "For helping you with the house—or for the kiss?" he inquired, teasing lights dancing through the depths of his eyes now.

Claire blushed. "For both, you impossible man. I never knew—" she stopped. It was far too dangerous to be revealing something like that.

"Neither did I," Elliot returned softly. He walked out into the foyer and to the door. "And it's going to get better and better, my sweet doubting Thomas. That I promise you."

As he opened the door he lifted the large manila envelope off the occasional table and held it out to her. "By the way, you need to get these forms filled out. My secretary would appreciate it if you could return them sometime next week. If you have any questions the number is on the envelope. If I'm not there Rhonda can answer." He chuckled at her look of utter bafflement. "See you soon, madam home designer."

He left, then stuck his head back in the door to order, "And no more marathon sessions at the drafting table, understand?" The door shut firmly this time, and a few minutes later Claire heard the sound of his T-bird growling to life and then fade away in the distance.

Claire tried all weekend to understand her reactions

to Elliot Ramsey, tried to understand her reactions to his kiss. She had been frightened, yes, taken aback as well, but she had also enjoyed it. There, she had admitted it at last.

She wanted him to kiss her again, when it boiled right down to the brass tacks of it, and she wanted to be drawn closer.

"Rubber baby buggy bumpers!" she muttered aloud, turning away from the window where she had seemed to spend most of the weekend and going down the hall through the door to her bedroom. She picked up the registration forms and literature from the nightstand by her bed. Should she just forget it? Should she back out now before things escalated beyond her ability to cope?

She had learned the hard way what her limits were, and still bore the scars. Elliot attracted her far more deeply than Gary ever had, probably because she was years older and wiser now, but that also meant the hurt she would sustain would be far more severe as well. Claire sank onto her narrow bed and closed her eyes. She couldn't stand all the pain again. She couldn't take the kind of chance required to open herself to loving a man.

God was sure to punish her for even trying, because after all hadn't she promised to love and honor Gary until . . . until death parted them? And hadn't she broken not only the vow to love and honor, but the very laws ordained by God Himself against even thinking evil thoughts about someone? Turning, she flung herself face down on the spread, confused and miserable.

What am I going to do? Mom, Dad . . . somebody . . . anybody . . . what am I going to do?

What she did do was retreat to her work once again. She finished the tracing for the house with the atrium and made the final copies on her blueprint machine. Mr. Davis was pleased, singing her praises with effusive embellishments and promises to give her cuttings from his plants. She accepted another job from a referral. She spent an afternoon with Mrs. Vancouver and her cousin, going over her plans and making recommendations for exterior paint colors. She wandered around the salesman's house and tried to take pride in its growing attractiveness, even managed to smile at one of the sparing compliments Chuck flung her way. She stayed so busy she couldn't think when she collapsed into bed at night, which was precisely the effect for which she had aimed.

With many misgivings she had gone ahead and completed all the forms, telling herself that at least she had gotten a very thorough physical and a good doctor out of it even if she did decide not to participate in the trek. The doctor had warned her about her excessive stress level, and when he found out the reason for the physical had concurred whole-heartedly.

"I've had quite a few people coming through here for one of Elliot's treks," he had told her. "It's a sound policy not to allow anyone to go until a physician gives the all-clear sign." He twinkled a smile at her over his horn-rimmed glasses. "Keeps my business perking right along, as well. Yes, you're definitely healthy enough to go on a Nature's Journeymen trek, Ms. Gerard, and in fact I hope you plan to start some preliminary exercising before. The symptoms of extreme fatigue and loss of appetite due to stress will undermine your stamina, and you'll definitely need that on one of those treks." He stood up, held out the completed form with his signature. "Let me hear how it went, and try not to work so hard between now and June."

Late one Friday evening Claire finally took the time to thoroughly read through all the literature Elliot had given her. The first meeting with the nine other people going on her trek was in the morning, and she wanted to learn as much as she could to avoid appearing any more muddled than she was already. No wonder Elliot wanted participants to have a good check-up first! While it was evident that he took great pains to make the treks as safe and well supervised as a nanny walking her charge for a stroll through the park, it was painfully evident after reading everything that a Nature's Journeymen trek was anything but a stroll in the park. Tramping about in the California Sierras for two weeks could not be compared in any way to her childhood hikes through the pine woods back in Georgia.

As Claire read and reread the list of potential hazards she had to fight a very different sort of fear. It was one thing to fear involvement with Elliot, but she had no desire to inadvertently involve herself with a startled skunk, male or female. She had even less desire to suffer hypothermia, blistered and infected feet, or a host of other tribulations designed to strike terror in the heartiest soul. In what moment of insanity had she decided backpacking sounded like a wonderful idea?

And yet, there was the promise of a glimpse of one of the many vanishing species of wildlife. There was the chance to listen to the wind in the trees, smell the evocative aroma of meadows and rich earthen forest floors, listen to the rushing water of clear, cold mountain streams . . . Elliot knew how to entice as well as issue warnings, Claire thought.

Her imagination had been kindled, and deep longing within stirred to uneasy life. Elliot had also maintained one of the main functions of Nature's Journeymen was for the participant to either come to know Jesus Christ on a personal level, or deepen a relationship already shared with Him. Claire was too confused to hope for anything like that, but she was beaten down enough to reach for a measure of peace. If Elliot could help her find her way to inner tranquility by leading her around the wilderness, then she had better forget her physical feelings for Elliot and her fears of the wilderness and go.

Saturday morning was a balmy May day redolent with salt and sea breezes and sunshine. Claire left all her windows open, and drove to Monterey with the car windows down, trying to allow the wind to clear her mind of all the cobwebs and shadowy doubts.

She was fifteen minutes early, but the large room at the motel was not empty. She stood on the threshold, gazing at a bewildering array of tents, backpacks, sleeping bags and other paraphernalia she was at a loss to identify. Over in a far corner were two men and another woman, and in spite of an unwelcome surge of shyness Claire picked her way slowly over to meet them.

"Hi," the girl spoke first, her voice friendly, eyes frankly curious. "You another one of the lucky ones going on Elliot's trek? I'm Page Parker, and these two sweeties are Rob Detweiler and Phil Markham." She slid a slender tanned arm through those of the men on either side of her, batting her large blue eyes with the ease of long practice. Blonde hair coiled in a casual knot atop her head, long legs encased in stovepipe jeans with a brief halter top above, Page Parker exuded an awareness of her attractiveness that Claire secretly admired.

She shook hands with the men, first with the slightly paunchy, slightly balding Rob Detweiler, who looked to be in his early forties, then with Phil Markham, a gangling young man with a thatch of hair almost as blond as Page's.

"I hope you all are as much of a novice as I am at all this," she ventured, covering up her usual reserve with a polite smile.

The two men laughed, and Page grinned. "Sweetie, we wouldn't be in a beginner's group if we weren't," she reminded Claire.

They all turned as voices from the side door heralded the arrival of more people. In another twenty minutes all ten had assembled, but there was still no sign of Elliot. Claire stood slightly aloof, watching everyone and absorbing personalities. Two of the other women were sisters, both unmarried and in their late forties; Claire was immediately drawn to their unaffected quiet friendliness.

The other female member of the trek was probably in her twenties like Page. She was a waitress at a fancy restaurant in Santa Cruz, and announced around a huge wad of chewing gum that she was "tired of alcohol and smoke and the smell of restaurant food and this ought to be a welcome change."

She only caught the name of one of the other men, a bearded, easy-going lawyer named Doug Tatum. One man she determined to avoid after his calculating eyes slid over her in an offensive manner. The other was a bean-pole teenager who scurried in the back door only a few minutes before Elliot strode briskly into their midst. Elliot flashed her a brief amused smile before encompassing everyone within his magnetic gaze.

"Let's get started right away." He herded them all over to the table where they had placed their paperwork. Motioning for them to pull chairs up, he dragged one over for himself and straddled it, resting his arms on the back. "It's going to be a long morning, and I'm sure you can all think of other things you'd rather be doing." White teeth gleamed briefly. "None of those things, I assure you, could be as important as this meeting." He reached for the stack of papers and scooped them up. "Everyone get all this stuff filled out?"

"I haven't had a chance to get my physical yet," the cocktail waitress replied, liquid brown eyes wide and unblinking. "But I promise I'll have it done before the trek."

Elliot had lifted his head from examining the papers

at her first words, and Claire caught her breath at the look on his face. She hoped she would never be caught beneath the piercing directness of that stare, and Donna, the waitress, even stopped chewing her gum. "Wasn't it made clear that you have your physical by this meeting?" he asked pleasantly enough, and Donna shrugged nervously.

"Yeah, well, it's hard to take time off with the hours I work, you know . . ."

He searched her face for a long minute, then stated flatly, "Have it to my secretary by next Wednesday or consider yourself out."

He scanned the circle of wary faces with a smile that did not hide the total implacability of his face. "Rule number one on this trek is that you *abide* by the rules. I'm in charge, and I expect absolute obedience. If any of you don't feel comfortable with that, or feel you're deserving of special consideration, let's talk about it now." He waited, unmoving, then nodded as Rob Detweiler indicated a question.

"Are we allowed to question a rule or order?" he queried in a mild tone, and the group relaxed slightly when Elliot grinned.

"Only after you obey it." He eyed the subdued Donna. "You've got to remember that I am going to be the only one with any experience, which means the responsibility for the safety of all ten of you rests with me. While the staff and I take every precaution and try to maintain a relatively controlled environment for you beginners, you are still out in the wilderness. There are no policemen, no firemen, no doctors, and for your well-being as well as mine I must have the assurance that you will do as I tell you. That's the only way to attain maximum benefits with minimum risk. I won't be asking you to do anything I wouldn't do myself, okay?"

"When you put it like that," Rob affirmed with a twinkle. "Speaking as one raw tenderfoot, I leave any decisions at the command level up to you."

Everyone laughed as Elliot mockingly sketched a salute, and the aura of tension eased. Claire pondered the man in front of her as he proceeded to tell them more about Nature's Journeymen, then turned to the teenaged young man and ordered him to start the introductions by giving them a brief autobiography. "We're going to be as close, perhaps even closer, than family for these two weeks," he reminded them all, "so let's use the few opportunities we have before then to become better acquainted."

For the next half hour Claire listened, marveling at the diversity of backgrounds and occupations. From cocktail waitress to lawyer, from accountant to home designer, this group of ten dissimilar people seemed a microcosm of the American marketplace. Because she was sitting off by herself, Claire's turn to share came last, and she wondered if she imagined the gleam of amusement in Elliot's eye when at last everyone focused directly on her. She gave the briefest account, blushing slightly as she was teased about her accent.

"Okay, then." Elliot rose, rubbing his palms together. "Let's get down to the nitty-gritty, which today consists of assigning you your equipment. I'm assuming you have all read the brochures, so you understand the feasibility of using Nature's Journeymen equipment on a beginner's trek. If—and of course I hope this is a very remote if—you decide backpacking is not for you, at least you won't be out hundreds of dollars' worth of equipment. On the other hand, if I succeed in converting you all—" he sent them a provocative look, "—if not to Christianity, then at least to backpacking, then this experience will enable you to buy your own gear with more confidence and discrimination. We'll start with the most important—your backpack."

He picked one up from the pile and proceeded to explain the reasons for the various straps and pockets and projections and differently sized frames. Then he instructed all the men to approach. "You might not be aware of the fact that the majority of backpacks are designed for a man's frame, which makes it relatively easy to find one that fits." With rapid, skillful movements he fit a backpack to each man, lifting and adjusting and then showing them how to arrange belts and shoulder straps for the most comfortable fit.

So intrigued was Claire by all the complexities that it took several moments to realize Elliot was measuring and fitting the women in the same manner as the men. Page and Donna were posturing and poking fun at Elliot, who teased them right back as he calmly lifted, adjusted, explained the difference in a woman's physiology (". . . beyond the obvious!" he had laughed) which necessitated a different kind of backpack. Claire hung back, allowing Josephine and Bessie Newman to go ahead of her. Could she stand quietly, without anyone noticing her—her fear and panic?

"Best for last?" Elliot quipped as she moved to stand in front of him, her eyes unwittingly betraying her turmoil. He lifted a backpack, murmuring as he held it up in front of her, "Relax, honey. Remember I've held you—and kissed you—and you came to no harm. This is no different, okay?" He slipped the straps over her arms, and as he fastened the hip belt his hands positioned the pack to rest properly just below her waist.

Claire closed her eyes, quivering at the sensations racing through her. Her hands were clenched to keep from raising them against his chest in protest . . . and need.

"Are you going to threaten me like Josephine did when I ask how much you weigh?" Elliot asked with a straight face as he began loading five-pound sandbags into the pack.

She lifted her gaze and reluctantly smiled. The easy-going, twinkling schoolteacher had tartly informed Elliot that her weight was none of his business and if he asked again she planned to drop a couple of the sandbags on his foot. "About a hundred and seven," Claire admitted quietly, her gaze dropping at Elliot's quick frown.

"You've lost some, haven't you?"

"Did Josephine ever tell you how much she weighed?" Claire hurriedly asked, avoiding answering his question.

"Of course." He began unfastening straps and then smoothly lifted off the backpack. "This one was too big for you," he told her as she opened her mouth to ask. "Your head would have been bumping the frame—this part here, see?" He tried another and Claire could immediately tell the difference.

"You're right!" she exclaimed, relaxing for the first time. "I can barely feel the thirty pounds—isn't that the weight I have to support?"

"Yes. I'll be interested to see your reaction after hiking for an hour or so over a rough trail." He removed the sandbags, then began unfastening the pack. "Claire . . . you need to put on a little weight and stop working so hard." When she wouldn't look at him he touched her chin, sighing at the reflexive flinch. He had so hoped she would be better by now. "Have you at least been walking a couple of miles every day?"

"Yes."

With a wry grimace he turned back to the others, allowing her the chance to compose herself. "All right, now, let's move to the sleeping bags. They're a little easier, and yes, they've all been thoroughly cleaned and sanitized . . ."

As the weeks passed Claire divided her time between work, walking, and reading. May melted into June, and her skin browned to a warm golden honey as her walks down the beach lasted longer and longer.

There were still dark circles under her eyes from working too late at night, and she hadn't gained any weight, but Elliot hadn't been able to yell at her because she hadn't seen him but once and then only for a few minutes.

He had dropped by the A-frame house the Redding's had chosen to have built, interrupting one of the workmen showing Claire samples of window and baseboard trim. "I'm on my way to Sacramento for a week," he told her. "I left something in your car I'd like you to read. There are several parts marked."

She had thought he had merely left more books or brochures on backpacking and braving the wilderness, and had been too caught up in learning about the many shapes of trim to even go over to her car and check. When she finally did she discovered that Elliot had only left one book, but it had nothing to do with backpacking. It was a Bible, brand-new and smelling of leather and fresh India paper, and her name was embossed in gold in the bottom right-hand corner.

Many times since, she had picked up the phone to call and either thank him, or scold him for such an extravagant gesture. She knew the Bible was an expensive one, and she knew he had chosen it with care. As he had told her, there were several passages marked, but Claire had read only one, the verses from Matthew he had quoted that memorable evening when he first kissed her. Somehow she couldn't bring herself to read any further after that.

She couldn't call Elliot, and she was relieved he hadn't called or come by himself. If they met again before she had a chance to recover her balance she would dissolve at his feet, spilling out her tortured confession as to why there was no use for her to read a Bible, or pray, or expect anything but harsh judgment from God.

She met with the nine other participants of the trek one other time, and learned how to set up, and then dismantle, her tent. Elliot was not there. Boyd Akins, an assistant, explained that Elliot was busy trying to tie up loose ends of his various architectural projects. Half the time he was out of town, and when he was in his office he had requested not to be interrupted. "And when Elliot says that, you listen," Boyd had shaken his head in wonder. "Beats me how a man can inspire the fear of the Lord without ever raising his voice, but Elliot does it."

Two nights before leaving, Claire tied up the last of her own loose ends. She had arranged for an answering service to take her calls, and had finished all the blueprints required before the end of June. The landlady who had leased her the house would stop in a couple of times to check up, and Elliot had a longstanding arrangement with the small Monterey airport where Nature's Journeymen members were allowed to leave their cars for a minimal fee. The only thing left to get ready now was herself.

She had carefully packed appropriate clothes, from the now broken-in tennis shoes and wool socks to the tentlike poncho issued for protection from rain. Elliot had explained that tennis shoes were sufficient since they would never be hiking longer than two hours, and that wool socks were better for the feet than cotton because wet cotton socks stayed wet, and thus caused blisters.

Her body was fairly tanned, so sunburn shouldn't be a problem if care was taken, and the lengthening walks had helped her stamina, she hoped. Her heart, on the other hand, was an unruly and feeble organ which ignored the firm dictates of her brain to behave in a calm, mature and professional manner. Excitement warred with fear of the unknown, the untried. The desire to see Elliot again was a restlessly prowling dragon, waiting to roar into flames the minute he spoke to her.

She had packed, with much misgiving, the Bible he

had given to her, although it had lain unopened by her bed these last weeks. Many times she had held it, rubbed her hands over the smooth black cover and smelled the newness of it as her fingers enjoyed its soft pliability. How she wished she could believe in it, and how she yearned for the comfort offered between the pages.

Elliot, she asked him over and over in silent supplication, *since you have such a good relationship with the Lord, could you put in a word for me?*

In the daytime she would laugh mirthlessly at this fancifulness, knowing she would never have the courage to ask such a question of Elliot, and knowing how useless it would be if she did.

It was the breathtaking photographs of the Sierras that sustained her, and the lure of the printed word describing their riches and wonders that kept her from backing down. She might never be granted inner peace or enjoy Elliot's close walk with Christ, and stark honesty impelled her to face a bleak future without further contact with Elliot Ramsey at all after the trek. But at least she could have the memory of the mountains, the knowledge that she had sojourned a spell with nature and emerged, if not a better person, at least a stronger one. And maybe, just maybe some of the crushing weight of guilt she bore could then be borne a little easier.

Nature's Journeymen Trek IIB began at dawn on a Saturday morning. Everyone met at the Monterey airport where they flew a small commuter prop to Modesto. From there a Nature's Journeymen bus would transport them to their drop-off point somewhere in Yosemite National Park.

"Don't look like that," Elliot had reassured with a grin when he had told them where they were going. "I know Yosemite conjures up pictures of hordes of tourists plodding and driving down Yosemite Valley to take pictures of Half Dome and El Capitan. But believe it or not ninety percent of the park is uncluttered wilderness and I'm taking you to a small portion of that ninety percent."

"Will we see any bears?" Bessie, Josephine Newman's sister, had asked nervously.

"I very much doubt it," Elliot promised, but there was a certain grim regret coloring his voice. "All the grizzlies were shot a long time ago, and the black bears tend to stick to the wildest sections where you won't be venturing as a beginner."

By the time Claire climbed onto a dusty, bedraggled-looking bus she had almost been infected by the enthusiasm and easy camaraderie of the others. There was a good deal of teasing and laughter about their beginner status.

As he climbed aboard the bus, Doug Tatum shot a look of mock horror at the grizzled bus driver. "Will this bucket of bolts make it up the mountain, or will we end up being just a part of the scenery instead of enjoying it?"

"She'll make it," the driver said slowly, his voice filled with laconic confidence. "I don't plan to break down somewhere on the road with a bunch of greenhorn tenderfoots."

They were barely seated when the bus snarled into life with a grumbling roar and grinding of gears, forcing them to grab wildly for handholds as it lurched forward onto the highway.

"Nice limousine!" Brad McAffe, the youngest member, called out, and no sooner had he said it than a chorus of laughter almost drowned out the noisy throb of the engine.

Claire sat by a window, her eyes glued to the countryside and her nerves throbbing along with the bus engine. It had begun. She was really going to be out in a totally new environment with nine strangers for two whole weeks.

All that stood between her and that vast wilderness was a man who had the ability either to strengthen her, care for her, and sustain her—or to destroy her completely. She was not only at the mercy of nature—whether he realized the fact or not—she was also at the mercy of Elliot Ramsey.

CHAPTER 6

THE COUNTRYSIDE STAYED FLAT for a few miles with huge orchards of almonds, walnuts, and peach trees flanking the road. In late June the trees were so heavy with fruit that long stakes had been propped up into the branches to keep them from collapsing. Gigantic irrigation systems provided the only water; some of the orchards were ankle-deep while around them was reflected the dry, dusty heat of a central California summer.

The road abruptly narrowed and became more winding as they entered the hills and valleys that preceded the entrance to the foothills of the Sierras. Dark green trees contrasted sharply with straw-colored grasses. As the land dipped into deep valleys and gently undulating hills, the green crops and orchards were replaced by a mixture of scrub and pin oaks.

It was all so different from the lush verdancy of the south with its azaleas and wisteria and flowering trees, its acres of either rich farmland or the infamous red clay. Claire sighed, a sound mingling joy with trepidation, tremulous hope with tremors of fear, while through the shimmering summer haze the California Sierras beckoned.

When the bus slowed to a crawl to cross a one-lane steel arch bridge over the Tuolumne River, everyone craned to see the dark green, smooth, fast-flowing water.

"I'd love to jump right out of this bus and into that," Page announced, wiping her hand across her brow.

"You'll get the chance," Elliot promised. He was sitting up front with the driver, but a good part of the time turned around to chat with the passengers. He had not singled Claire out, although her heart had jerked in a pleased little spasm at the warm look he had bestowed upon her at the Monterey airport. Since then he had not spoken beyond issuing general instructions and a teasing aside or two such as he favored any of the others with. Claire hoped this neutral attitude was to keep her from feeling awkward, and was annoyed with herself for the twinge of hurt that kept jabbing whenever he joked and clowned so naturally with the others.

"I better warn you," he shouted so all could hear, "that what looks so cool and refreshing is in reality cold enough to freeze your toes if you're not careful."

"There had to be a catch," Page grumbled, tossing her head and scowling at Elliot as she batted her lashes with teasing coyness. "Will you keep me warm, Mr. Ramsey?"

"I'd be glad to see you in the warmest spot by the fire," Elliot shot back unfazed.

"I'd be glad to warm *you* up," a voice announced in a silken murmur above Claire, and she turned to stare up at Michael Wolfe, the computer salesman from Oakland.

Claire had avoided him on the few previous meetings with their group. He was a little too friendly, a little too pleased with his curly brown hair and muscular build. Other women might find him attractive, but Claire was not other women.

"I don't plan to need warming up," she declared flatly, then deliberately turned her head back toward the window.

Don't sit down, she begged him silently.

"Hey, Mike, doing okay back here?" With careless ease Elliot clapped him on the shoulder, then dropped onto the seat by Claire. "Haven't had a chance to see how you're holding up, Claire. Everything all right? Enjoying the view?"

She turned back around and forced a smile. "It's marvelous. I can't wait until we get there."

Michael dropped down in the seat across from them, his own smile forced. "I'm not so sure I'm looking forward to a two-hour hike with sixty pounds on my back."

"Now, what's a healthy, strapping young man like you doing complaining about our first hike?" Josephine grinned at him from the seat in front of Claire.

As they began bantering back and forth Claire felt her tense muscles gradually relaxing. She sneaked a shy glance up at Elliot, and found him studying her with compassion.

"Okay?" he asked softly, and when she nodded, his hand reached out to briefly cover hers. "Good. Don't worry, Claire. I'm going to take care of you."

He rose. "All right, gang. Coulterville's just ahead. We'll stop for gas, and you have your last chance at civilization for two weeks. You've got five minutes."

They were standing in a small clearing, listening without moving for a minute to the receding roar of the bus. The air was clear and clean and warm, and the sun streamed down through a covering of sentinel-straight sugar pines. It streamed down as well onto the jumbled mass of equipment, which after a last collective sigh, the group turned to confront. Elliot commandeered Brad and Mike to help organize, and in another short while everyone was shouldering his fully loaded backpack for the first time. Claire remembered the session where they had worn them filled with the sandbags for an hour. Elliot was right. It was definitely going to be interesting after two hours.

The first thirty minutes her body spent adjusting to the unfamiliar weight as her senses reveled in the surroundings. It was quiet except for the shuffle of footsteps and the sound of labored breathing, for there was almost a reverent stillness which precluded conversation. A nuance of wind brushed the upper boughs of the trees, and every now and then a bird twittered.

Rob Detweiler, the balding accountant, gave out first. "It's humiliating, of course," he panted as he mopped his streaming brow with an already soaked handkerchief, "but I'm hoping to have improved my status in fourteen days."

Elliot prowled among their sprawled bodies, checking packs and pulses and smiling at the slapstick humor permeating his already tired charges. He squatted in front of Claire, his eyes taking in her flushed cheeks and damp, windblown hair plastered to her forehead. "How many miles a day did you tell me you walked?" he asked, picking up her wrist with the same efficient care he had Donna's, Rob's, and the Newman sisters'.

"Two or three." Claire controlled her breathing with grim determination, avoiding his very direct stare.

Elliot pondered the bent head a minute. "Hmm . . ." was all he eventually observed, however.

Catching Josephine's lifted brow, he nodded his head a millimeter, then so swiftly Claire did not have time to flinch he lifted her to her feet.

"Five minutes is up. Let's go. We have over an

hour left and a campsite to set up before dark. Rob, Donna, I want you two and Claire to walk behind me so I can keep a closer eye on the three of you.''

"What about me?" Page called plaintively. "Aren't I close enough to dead yet?" Everyone laughed, good humor restored as the group resumed hiking single-file down the narrow, winding path.

For an hour they hiked, until even Brad ran out of breath for telling jokes and making sassy comments on everybody's lack of fitness. Donna moaned about her back and shoulders, and Page griped about her feet. Phil longed for a tall, cool drink, and Doug gasped that he'd settle for a short warm one at this point. Rob and the Newman sisters were red in the face and perspiring heavily, but in spite of being the oldest members of the trek, they maintained a stoic determination not to complain. Claire admired them for that, and strove to do likewise, although her lungs were on fire and, like Donna, her back and shoulders were screaming in protest.

She was concentrating so hard on just keeping her balance and putting one foot in front of the other that at first her weary brain did not register the sound of a real scream. She bumped into Donna, then lifted her head and turned around.

"Look at it! It's awful! Ugh! Get rid of it, Elliot!" Page shuddered and clung to an amused Doug, losing all her sophisticated poise and casual elegance.

"It doesn't like you anymore than you like it," Elliot crouched down at Page's feet. "And contrary to all the horror movies, tarantulas are not the deadly, vicious lot you might think."

"A tarantula!" Brad, enthusiasm and youthful exuberance overcoming caution, pushed away from the sapling where he had been leaning, lost his balance, and careened into Claire, who had started to walk back to see as well. Tired and unused to the unwieldy weight of the backpack, she fell heavily and with scant grace, scraping her palms raw as she tried to break the momentum.

"We've got one down, Elliot!" Rob called as he tried to help Claire to her feet, his round face lined with concern.

The tarantula forgotten, Elliot was by her in a flash, gently easing her to a sitting position by the side of the trail. He loosened the hip strap, then without a word lifted her hands, his mouth tightening at the raw, oozing palms.

"I'm all right," Claire promised faintly, trying to ease Brad's distress.

"Gosh, I'm sorry, Claire," he apologized, his face beet-red. "It's just that I'd never seen a tarantula before."

"Don't worry about it, Brad," Elliot was shrugging off his own pack as he spoke. "Could have happened to anybody." He found a square metal box, from which he drew out a tube of ointment. Turning back to Claire, he smiled directly into her eyes as he took note of her own discomfort at the ring of faces all peering down anxiously. At that moment Claire almost wished the gargantuan hairy spider would effect a re-appearance. She hated being the center of attention.

"Listen, people," Elliot pointed out calmly. "You'll be seeing far worse than a scraped palm or two over the next two weeks." He briefly scanned the group. "Hopefully not too much worse—I'd hate to have to use my short-wave radio to summon a chopper after two years of no emergencies. Why don't you all take advantage of the break, and slip off your packs. I'll give you ten minutes while I see to Claire."

He waited for them to obey, then turned to her. She was exhausted, he could tell. Exhausted yet determined to maintain her poise. Not once in the last hour and a half had she uttered a word, and the frequent glances he had thrown over his shoulder had gone unnoticed. Donna had gamely managed to smile through her complaining, and Rob would give him a thumbs-up sign, but for the last forty minutes Claire had doggedly kept her head down, shoulders bent from the weight of the pack as she walked.

Elliot knew a surge of protection, pride, and concern so strong it fairly rocked him back on his heels. For two cents he'd chuck all his rules and regulations and relieve her of the pack, just to ease her physical discomfort. A muscle twitched in his jaw as he mentally viewed the ensuing disorder that would follow such a rash action on his part.

He wanted Claire out here with a need bordering on desperation, but he hadn't realized how hard it would be to watch the toughening-up process on her. Donna's and Page's struggles did not move him at all because he knew it was all just part of growing, a necessary step to a better awareness of personal strength and limits. The drooping, fragile female in front of him looked as if she had just about reached her limit, however, and he could only hope and pray he could buoy Claire up for the remaining few miles to camp.

"I guess you win the first merit badge," he teased while he applied the antiseptic cream. As Elliot hoped, she raised heavy lids and gazed up into his face. Her eyes were the nutty brown of the forest floor, dulled by fatigue and discomfort.

"Merit badge?" she repeated, the merest glimmer of green flecking the brown depths.

Elliot held her hands palms up, noting with a hot stab of triumph that she wasn't flinching away from his touch. "On beginner's treks I've often thought it would be a good idea to hand out badges for casualties instead of accomplishments," he informed her with a half-grin. "They seem to encounter so many more of the former that receiving a badge might help counteract the humiliations endured. What do you think? If I had a badge to pin on you would that make the pain in your hands go away?"

The laughter started as a flicker and spread until her tired mouth lifted into a smile.

"How about giving out kisses?" Page suggested. "Isn't that what parents do when their kid scrapes a knee? I know I'd forget all my aches and pains if you kissed me better, Elliot."

Claire stiffened instantly, jerking her hands free, and Elliot restrained his frustration with great effort. Page Parker was a tease and a flirt, but she had a basically kind heart and had no way of knowing about Claire's hypersensitivity to any mention of physical closeness. Only why did she have to choose this particular moment?

"That might work for women, but if he tried to kiss my hand I'd be more likely to feed him my fist," Doug Tatum joked, and everyone laughed.

Elliot waited by Claire until he saw her relax, then with easy matter-of-factness helped her to stand, shrug back into her pack, and tighten the straps. When she started to thank him he hushed her, grinned, and tapped her nose with his forefinger. "Just make it to camp for me, that's all the thanks I ask."

The campsite was situated beneath a stand of massive ponderosa pines and a few scattered white fir. The ground was a thick carpet of pine needles, although a stone's throw away an outcropping of glacier-worn rock and stubble formed a miniature mountain, with only a few brave white firs thrusting their way upwards toward the sky. A few gray logs, worn smooth by the ravages of time, had been carefully arranged in a semicircle off to one side, and Michael quickly pointed this fact out.

"I have an arrangement with the park," Elliot reminded him. "Since beginner treks have to be so carefully controlled, and since the idea is to get as far away from civilization as possible without unduly endangering your lives, the places available for treks

99

are limited. Thus, I do use the same spot on more than one trek. At least take comfort in the fact that you're the first group of the season to camp here."

"If the park is so big, why can't you take people to different places every time?" Donna asked. Everyone had quickly shed their packs and were lying in a state of pleasant exhaustion waiting for their feet to quit throbbing and their backs to recover sufficiently to set up the camp.

Elliot, on the other hand, was not even breathing hard. He answered Donna while he began unpacking his own gear. "The beginner treks need to be confined to the lower levels, an area known as the Transition Zone. The weather isn't as harsh, the conditions less forbidding, and since the altitude doesn't go beyond nine thousand feet—and we won't be going over five—you don't encounter problems with altitude sickness."

He began collecting large stones for the central campfire, continuing to talk as he worked. "There are all sorts of trails already well defined, in spite of strenuous efforts to leave the wilderness as we find it. So . . . when you combine all these factors you end up with a very small space in which to take a group of inexperienced people for two weeks of wilderness living."

He finished placing another stone and stood, surveying the group with solemn eyes. "Remember, one of the reasons you came on the trek was to learn how to live with nature without destroying or unduly disturbing it. It's impossible to always disguise the mark of man, but if we all pitch in and do our part you'll still be able to—as one of the brochures puts it—put your finger on the pulse of nature and feel her breathe." He stretched, inhaling deeply and closing his eyes a moment.

"You can also find time to be still and come to know God. I hope and pray for that, although as I told you at the very first meeting no one is obliged to listen when I share my faith. You're free to do nothing more than enjoy the solitude—just as I am free to talk about my Christian experience."

Elliot picked up Phil's backpack and dumped it on his chest. "Time to get to work, now. The sun will be setting in about two hours and we have a lot to do."

In the next hour the gear was unloaded and the tents set up. Elliot allowed them to choose their own spots, although he cautioned them to make sure the area was free of sticks, pinecones and other debris, and that their tent was in sight of his own which he had erected near the center of the camp. He moved from one member to the other, helping with the fiberglass poles and brown nylon fabric that metamorphosed into compact dome tents.

"Well, it was different back in Monterey!" Donna protested sheepishly when Elliot patiently showed her again how to put it up, even though Boyd had done so three times on the Saturday they had met to learn about their tents.

Claire chose a spot as far away from the others as she felt Elliot would allow her. She was feeling a bewildering surge of claustrophobia, surrounded by people who still were virtual strangers. It was rapidly sinking in that part of the learning experience out here was not only how to enjoy nature and appreciate solitude; she had to learn the basics of communal living as well.

As she fumbled gamely with her tent, ignoring her stinging, burning palms, her mind grappled for a semblance of its former control. Elliot had said he would take care of her, hadn't he? She had trusted him this far—she would have to learn to trust him with the future. Could she?

"Thought you could use some help with your tent."

Michael had strolled up so silently she hadn't heard, and at the sound of his voice right at her shoulder Claire gasped and jumped back.

"I can manage fine, thank you," she told him, turning with deliberate movement to unzip the outer flap covering the doorway.

"Your hands look pretty sore, you know. I thought I'd offer my assistance while you rested and told me how marvelous and thoughtful I was." He smiled a deliberate, inviting smile, then stepped in front of the door, reaching to pick up her hand where it was stretched out on the zipper. Claire backed away as if he had just burst into flames and he stared at her in consternation.

"What's the matter with you? I'm just trying to help, not attack you." He followed her retreat, and Claire watched helplessly as a predatory flare leaped into his narrowed eyes. "You've bugged me ever since that first Saturday with your touch-me-not look daring me to get too close. I never could resist a challenge . . ."

"I'm not challenging you." Claire glanced around. Elliot was occupied on the other side of the clearing with Bessie; the nearest tent to Claire's was Page's, and she was talking with Phil and Doug as they stored some of the food inside the cooking pots. "And I told you I don't need any help. Since there is nothing left to do, why don't we go help with the food?"

"I'd rather talk to you. Is it just me, or are you this standoffish with every guy you meet?" He was still stalking her, and every time Claire took a step backwards he followed.

Claire could feel the old panic filling her, the horrifying desperation that rendered her limbs useless and her brain a lump of soggy cotton. She knew she was behaving irrationally, that the man in front of her was only trying to be friendly. He was not going to hurt her, force her . . .

"Please just leave me alone." It was no use. Her voice had cracked, and now he knew what a spineless coward she was. She stared into his scowling face like

102

a baby bird caught in a snare, willing her spine to stiffen, her hands to stop trembling.

"Claire?" Elliot appeared from behind one of the massive pines, his countenance altering at the sight of Claire's motionless form. He glanced at Michael, and was at Claire's side with a silent speed that was deceptively casual. "Mike, did you help her with her tent? I see it's up."

"She did it herself." He looked from one to the other. "Don't come too close, Ramsey. She might freeze you." He turned and strode over to the other two younger men and Page, hands stuffed in the hip pockets of his jeans.

Claire dragged her gaze away from his retreating back to look up at Elliot. "I'm being a fool," she confessed, her traitorous voice cracking again. "He . . . he said he . . . he only wanted to help."

"Take it easy, honey. Come on, let's see how you did with your tent, then I'll check your hands and deliver a lecture." He waited, not touching her, until she slowly moved back toward her tent, though his arms ached with the effort to restrain himself from pulling her into his embrace. "Hmm . . . not bad, even if it is a little lopsided. Did you remember to check the ground first?"

Claire nodded. She couldn't speak because of the lump choking her throat from Elliot's offhand manner. But then, what else did she have the right to expect? If he went around babying every female on his treks he'd never get anything else done. Just because he had held her and kissed her and awakened feelings in her she never knew existed didn't mean *he* had felt anything special.

"Claire."

All of a sudden his hand was cupping her chin and lifting her face. It was so warm, so firm and strong . . . yet so gentle that she wanted to butt into it and mew like a homeless kitten. Her eyes were wide and

103

unblinking, focusing on the unruly lock of black hair falling like a misplaced comma over his forehead.

"My confused, scared dream designer . . ." His voice spilled over her like an unction, soothing and tender. "I'd like nothing better at this moment than to take you in my arms and shoulder all your burdens like I did one precious other time . . . and then treasure your mouth like I did for one precious moment." His other hand lifted to caress her fragile cheekbone, then dropped back to his side. "But not only are we surrounded by people, I'm the guy in charge, my sweet one, and that means I have to stay on top of things. If I started kissing you I wouldn't notice if a whole pack of bears descended and made off with all the supplies, not to mention nine helpless people."

"Elliot . . ." Her face suffused with rich color and her mouth broke open in a real smile at last. "You say the most outrageous things."

"That's true. I did say there weren't any bears around here, didn't I?" He released her chin so he could trace her jaw and the line of her throat before forcefully stuffing his hand into the waistband of his jeans. There was a satisfied smile on his face as she gave in to the laughter. "That's my girl," he said very softly, then nodded his head in the direction of the rest of the camp.

"Now, I want you to come on over with the rest and relax. No one—*no one*, Claire—is going to intimidate or threaten you in any way. I want you to open yourself up, give to others the Claire Gerard I've been privileged to glimpse on too few occasions." He paused, then added with fervent emphasis, "That's the first step in becoming a new person. Soon, I pray, you'll learn to open yourself up even more, and let the love of Christ turn you into a new creature entirely."

Claire wondered how his prayers could possibly help her, but she also found herself wondering if maybe Elliot Ramsey's prayers just might be powerful enough to make a difference.

Evening descended first with blazing colors that streaked the sky, fading rapidly to the softer magenta, violet rose and then finally a deep, soft black matte sprinkled with sugar stars. The group sat around the campfire, basking in the crackling odor of smoke and wood, the fragrant aroma of pine in the clean air. They had managed to survive their first experiences of cooking on their portable kerosene stoves, learned the mechanics of cleaning up without using soap, and were gradually beginning to function as a group. Elliot had promised them a chance to bathe in a nearby stream tomorrow, but for now everyone chose to ignore one of the baser facts of life in the wilderness.

"This is simply delightful," sighed Josie, who was sitting between her sister and Claire. She stretched her compact, sturdy frame and grinned across at Page, who was slumped with her back against one of the logs. "I think trifles like deodorant and perfume can be easily ignored at times like this, don't you agree, Page?"

Page lifted one arm half-heartedly in response. "The people who work at the office with me might disagree, but right now I'm too wiped out to care what I smell like."

"You mean you didn't bring along your bottle of Giorgio?" Doug teased her lazily. Every time the group had gotten together, Page's favorite perfume always permeated the air.

"What about you, Claire?" Michael prodded. His voice was teasing, too, but Claire stiffened at the nuance of malice snaking beneath the lighter tones. "Did you bring along your favorite scent? Let's see if I can guess what it is—something cool, forbidding and mysterious, right?"

"I don't wear perfume," Claire revealed with a dry smile.

"Who needs it when we have all this fresh air anyway," Doug smiled over at Claire, the gleam of teeth within his beard genuine and easy. "What's on the agenda for tomorrow, O fearless leader?" He turned to speak to Elliot, who had been patrolling the site to make sure the food sacks were securely suspended, tents in place and stoves cleaned and put away.

"I plan to have two organized hikes each day, but other than that your time is your own. Just remember the most important rule as beginners here is to always tell me where you're going—and never go farther out than the sound of my voice." He sat down and surveyed the group of faces dimly lit by the fire's flickering light. "The first day or two you'll probably all suffer from acute boredom and an overdose of the burning desire to do something, go someplace, accomplish some worthwhile project."

"Not me," piped in Donna. "I don't plan to do anything but nothing."

"Actually," Elliot assented, "that's precisely the idea. I would have stated it a little differently, though. Something along the line of 'Be still, and know that I am God . . .' I always tend to think in Psalms when I'm out here."

"I like that, Elliot," Josie commented. "In fact, I think I'll use the Psalms as a reference for my devotionals while we're out here."

"How about having some group devotionals?" Phil suggested, ignoring the snort from Michael as well as the uncomfortable shifting by Brad.

"Sure. Set them up with anyone who's interested."

"And if you're not?" Michael inserted, his voice mocking.

Elliot shrugged, his own countenance in the firelight unperturbed. "That's fine, too. Remember, being a Christian is not a requirement for these treks, even though it's the 'sole' requirement for the ones taking place in heaven." He stood. "I think we better pack it in, folks, before the mosquitoes get too bad and Rob falls asleep here by the fire. Make sure you keep your flashlights handy, and that your tent flaps are securely fastened. Shake your sleeping bags before you get in them, and do the same things for your shoes in the morning. You should be protected in your tents, but let's not take any chances."

Claire had changed into her thin cotton nightgown and was just lifting the sleeping bag to slide in when she heard Elliot softly call her name. She crawled to the flap and unzipped it a little.

"What is it?" she asked, her voice uncertain.

"I thought I'd stop by and say goodnight. At least when it's pitch dark outside I don't have to worry about everyone spying on us."

Claire bit her lip to hold back a smile.

"I also wanted to ask if you brought the Bible I gave you." The teasing note was gone now, and Claire swallowed heavily.

"Yes, I brought it, Elliot," she managed at last. "I–I never have really thanked you. I didn't quite know how."

"You don't have to thank me."

His voice caressed her with fingers of tenderness that made her want to throw open the flap and fling herself into his arms. What on earth was the matter with her? For over eight years now she had dreaded, yes, feared, any man's touch, yet her body was clamoring for just that. Only not just any man—but Elliot. What had he done to her? How had he surmounted her formidable barriers and undermined all her hard-won resolve?

For hours afterward she wondered whether it was the betrayal of her own body, or the dramatic circumstances and concealing cover of darkness that made her blurt out the words. "Elliot, I'm so afraid of you. Of how you make me feel. What am I going to do?"

As she spoke she closed her eyes in agony, wishing she could melt into the pineneedled forest floor and never see him again. The silence following her impetuous outburst was deafening.

"Honey. . ." The word whispered into her ear like a sigh. "Open your flap a minute and look at me while I talk to you."

"It's too dark to see." She protested. "And I'm not dressed."

She heard a muffled sound that might have been laughter, and she blushed. "What are you wearing, Claire?"

"My nightgown. What else?" Her voice was bewildered now, and she clutched her arms to her sides as if to prevent any further unwise revelations from spilling forth.

"You don't remember my advice to just wear a T-shirt so you could dress at a moment's notice?"

There was a dreadful pause before Claire could bring herself to confess, "I—felt too—exposed."

"Ah . . . Claire . . ." The words trailed away into soft laughter. "Don't move. I'll be right back."

Stunned into acquiescence, Claire did exactly as he requested, and hadn't moved a muscle when she heard Elliot return.

"I've got something for you," he announced, laughter still lacing the words. "I've turned off my flashlight, so you can open the flap and take it."

Claire obeyed, and found herself holding an overly large Nature's Journeymen T-shirt.

"Slip it over your gown and then open your flap all the way. Please, Claire. I need to talk to you for just a minute. That's all, I promise. I'm not going to scare you any more. In fact, I'm hoping this will help ease your fears."

She couldn't help herself. For over a month now she had hoped, yearned, dreamed that Elliot would pursue whatever he had started the night he kissed her and promised her things would only get better. Her mind might warn her away, and her heart knew that she was only opening herself up to more hurt, but the power Elliot wielded was far greater than her guilt and fear. With shaking hands she pulled the T-shirt over her head, and then unzipped the flap.

CHAPTER 7

IN THE COMPLETE OBSCURITY of the night he was nothing more than a dark shape waiting motionless at the door of her tent. Claire peered through the darkness, straining to see his face, the expression in his eyes. She could hear the sound of his steady breathing, and smell the strangely pleasing scent of his maleness mingling with the smoke and pine.

When he didn't speak or immediately move, she spoke instead, her voice a breathless whisper of sound. "Elliot? What did you want?"

A sigh floated past her ear. "I did—and do—want a lot of things, and I'm having a dickens of a time with one of them in particular."

"What one is that?"

"I want to hold you, Claire. I want to hold you and protect you and imbue you with—" he stopped, then exhaled in a warm puff of air and finished simply, "with the same desire for me I feel for you. But I'm not going to until you're ready, honey, so please don't scramble back into the tent and curl up into a defensive little ball. Remember, I promised you I had an answer to help ease your fears."

Claire took one step forward, coming so close to Elliot she could feel the heat from his body. She was shivering, not just from the brisk night air but from a tingling, fearful sense of excitement. Her legs were separate entities moving independently of the rest of her, but she was driven by the same overpowering force that had unzipped the tent flap. Besides, it was dark, wasn't it?

"I told you I was afraid of the way you make me feel, Elliot," she managed in a level voice, "mainly because I'm *not* scrambling back into my tent. I–I don't want to, as long as . . . as long as . . ." Her sense of preservation finally nudged out her brief display of bravery as she floundered to a halt.

"As long as I behave?" Elliot prompted.

His hand was suddenly—and with disturbing accuracy—cupped about her chin, the fingers stroking with tender movements. Claire quit breathing and swayed forward with unconscious grace.

"As long as you behave like this," she whispered, the confession, a susurration of sound that hovered in the awesome stillness. Her eyes closed, and she waited with the lassitude of a man waiting for the guillotine to fall, helpless in the face of a reality too overwhelming to fight. In truth she was too tired to fight, too stunned by the depth of her response to Elliot. He could kiss her, or hold her, and she wouldn't be able to pull away. If he did neither . . . something inside of her would wither and die.

"Claire," he groaned, and then, "God, help me . . ." as he pulled her into his arms and his mouth came down on hers.

He kissed her with deep warmth and restrained passion, holding her close without demanding anything beyond the sweet compliancy of her body. It was the most difficult thing he had ever done in his life. He could feel the desire in her warring with the fear, and though she was yielding, she was not giving

111

back. It was almost as if she did not know how, and yet she was thirty years old. With a last tender touch of his lips on hers he finally lifted his head, one hand holding her head against his shoulder while the other stroked up and down her back and arms, calming, gentling her.

"Oh . . . Elliot . . ." she sighed, moving her head against the solid wall of his chest to gaze up into the opaque shadows and contours of his face. "What have you done to me?"

The ghost of a laugh ruffled her dark hair. "What have you done to me?" he returned, hugging her close and then releasing her with obvious reluctance. "We cannot do this, my love. Not here, not now. It's not right—and I want you to trust me."

"But . . . but I do." Her voice was bewildered, and Elliot smiled over her head.

"And I thank God for it, but I want you to trust me in the daytime as well, and to do that you've got a lot of other problems in your life you need to face first." Elliot placed his hands on her shoulders. "I came over here tonight to ask you to read a certain passage out of your Bible. I'm glad you brought it with you, Claire."

"I wanted to, but Elliot—" she bit her lip, then blurted out, "I haven't been able to read it."

His hands squeezed her shoulders reassuringly. "That's okay, honey, You're going to be able to now, because out here surrounded by God's handiwork it's a whole lot easier. And I want you to start with the seventy-seventh Psalm."

"The seventy-seventh Psalm," she parroted obediently, but her mind was whirling in confusion, in an upsurge of panicked despair. Could she share her past now, here in the dark, after they had shared such an unforgettable moment together? What would he say, how would he react? Would he shudder in disbelief, disillusionment, and never touch her again? The pain

112

almost doubled her over, and Elliot immediately felt the tension.

"Honey, what's the matter? I'm not trying to back you into a corner, or even force my faith on you, Claire. I'm only asking you to give it a try, for my sake—and because here in the dark you've claimed you trust me. Claire?"

Her body drooped as if his hands on her shoulders were weights of iron. She would not tell him right now. She could not. She would read the passage he requested, and then perhaps when she wasn't so tired, so confused, so utterly vulnerable she would confess the unforgivable nature of her sins. "I'll read it, Elliot."

Dear Father in heaven, why did she sound so defeated, so despondent? Why is she just as afraid of You as she is of me, Lord?

"There's a particular verse I want you to try and take hold of, Claire," he instructed now, letting go of her and reaching to open the flap. "You have a certain expression on your face sometimes that wrenches my heart, a look of hopelessness and dejection, like you're crying out inside only you're afraid to let it show. Like the only songs in the night you ever sing are sad and lonely ones." His hand came out one last time to feather down her cheek. "Read the psalm for me, and learn that you are not the only one who has a song in the night, my lost and hurting lamb."

Long after he had left, and there were no other sounds but the wind in the trees and the occasional cry of an owl, no other light but the far-off glitter of the stars, Claire lay in her sleeping bag with flashlight and Bible. Her mind was struggling to grasp the immensity of the words she had read, the unmistakable fact that right here in the Bible were words she herself might have written. Someone else, eons ago, had cried out in despair to God. Someone else had borne intolerable burdens . . . and yet they had still cried out to God. Had God listened then?

How had Elliot come to pick this particular passage for her to read? How could he possibly have managed to probe way beyond the barriers she had erected and see straight into her tormented soul? How had he known? She fell at last into exhausted sleep, her hand still resting on the opened Bible.

Groans and moans permeated the campsite the first morning.

"I never knew improving my awareness of nature would hurt so much," Page moaned as she massaged suntan oil on her bared legs.

"I thought waitressing was backbreaking work," Donna added. She and Phil Markham were playing tic-tac-toe in the dirt, and she giggled as he pushed her playfully. "I'll never complain about those trays again."

Claire was sitting with Josephine and Bessie at the edge of the campsite, enjoying the clear morning with its play of sunshine and shadow over the ridges and peaks of the mountains, the dew-washed freshness of the trees and meadows in front of them.

"How are your hands this morning, Claire?" Bessie inquired with motherly concern. She was the flightier of the two sisters, but so amiable and kindhearted it was easy to overlook her tendency to gush. "That was a nasty spill you took yesterday. I must say Josephine and I were quite concerned about your being able to make it to camp."

"She managed fine, though." Josie, as everyone but her sister called her, smiled fondly at Claire. "I rather imagine any respectable female would have managed fine if Elliot looked at them the way he looked at you." She stretched back, resting her hefty weight on her hands as she looked up at the bright blue sky. ". . . or unrespectable females, for that matter," she added, pretending not to notice Claire's discomfort. "I'll be interested to see how he handles

Page over the next two weeks. That gal's got her eye on him, I can tell you."

"My goodness, how she loves to flirt!" Bessie nodded vigorously, cocking her fuzzily curled head and eyeing Claire. "Didn't Elliot say he knew you before the trek, Claire? Are the two of you sweethearts? He seems a nice enough man, and a decent Christian, mind you, but you ought to be careful all the same, way up here with no protection."

"Leave the poor child alone, Bessie," Josie ordered with a good-natured chuckle. "The way you chatter on she'll be hiding out the entire two weeks in her tent."

Claire, her face a delicate shade of rose, toyed with a massive pinecone the size of a pineapple. She had been amazed and delighted with them, marveling at the difference in sizes compared to the modest pinecones back in Georgia. Right now she felt as prickly as the object she was holding.

"I have met Elliot before," she admitted, standing abruptly when his voice suddenly called out from the center of camp, demanding everyone's presence. "I guess we better see what he wants."

She hurried back through the trees, missing the satisfied looks the Newman sisters exchanged.

"I thought we'd organize our first morning hike, let you work up a good sweat, and then you can have your first bath in a mountain stream," Elliot told his charges when they were all assembled. Today he was wearing shorts with a faded Nature's Journeymen T-shirt, and Claire couldn't help remembering the garment she had carefully folded away an hour before. Did he give them away to women on every trek?

"Do we have to go on a hike?" Rob questioned with a smiling grimace. "I feel muscles I never knew I had and wish I didn't after the hike we endured yesterday to get us to this supposed paradise."

There was a chorus of assents and laughing derision until Elliot held up a hand.

"The hikes are not mandatory, I told you. But I will point out that more exercise will loosen up all those protesting muscles, whereas sitting around is only going to make you stiffen more." He grinned an easy, cajoling grin. "It's only an hour or so this time, and you don't have to carry a full pack. As your more knowledgeable leader I strongly recommend it, but the final decision is yours. We leave in ten minutes."

He moved over to Claire. "Let's have a look at your hands this morning, Claire. We need to keep them clean, remember?"

She held them up without speaking, hoping no one would comment on their trembling. Elliot, by accident or design, had moved so that she was blocked from view, although out of the corner of her eye she could see Michael's knowing smile. The rush of feeling that swooshed through her as his fingers gently examined the tender palms almost caused her to close her eyes.

"Do they still hurt?" he asked her, his eyes showing concern as he watched her struggling to compose her features.

"Not much."

It's just you, she wanted to confess. *It's your touch, the way you look at me. I think I might be falling in love with you, Elliot Ramsey.* The words sprang into her brain with such spontaneous revelation that for one horrible moment she was afraid he could read it in her face. She had avoided emotional entanglements with religious fervor for so long that she had been completely blind-sided, so secure had she been in the impervious condition of her heart.

"My hands are fine," she said firmly, though she dropped her gaze to the ground.

"They look pretty raw, still. You shouldn't have put your tent up alone, Ms. Independence. Come over here and let me put some more antibiotic cream on them before the hike."

He started off toward his tent, then paused and

116

glanced back over his shoulder. "You are coming on the hike, aren't you?"

"I guess you're caught now, aren't you, Claire?" teased Doug as he walked by on the way to his own tent. "Come on, you'll enjoy it."

"Did you sleep at all?" Elliot asked when they were at his tent and out of earshot of the others. He was rubbing in the ointment with careful fingers, but his eyes were searching hers. "Your eyes still look tired, and the shadows are still there."

He put the cream back in the medical kit and then stood there, arms folded across his chest as he pondered her. "Are you upset about last night?" he murmured, and there was enough anxiety in the question for Claire to stutter reassurances.

"Oh, no, I'm not upset, Elliot. It was wonderful—I mean, I . . . I . . . how did you pick the Bible verses you did?" she finally stammered and watched the slow grin inching across his face and the anxiety melting to satisfaction.

"You do have the most endearing blush, Ms. Gerard," he informed her, the tones low and caressing. "And it was easy to pick that psalm—it had your name written across the top, don't you agree?"

"But how did you know I felt like that?" She had to know, had to understand what it was about Elliot that allowed him to understand her so well. She kept her eyes glued to his face, wondering at the strange array of expressions.

"I've told you before that I care about you," he finally answered carefully. "Also that I've been praying for you. You might not accept this, but I believe God led me to that psalm for the specific purpose of leading you to it." His eyes burned with conviction, an inner fire of faith that Claire was convinced would never be doused. "I believe you can find the answers in the Bible, Claire, and through praying. If you haven't learned either of those yet,

117

then trust me to teach you. Just as you trusted me last night with your feelings.''

He glanced over Claire's shoulder, and some of the burning intensity faded from his eyes. "You ready to go, Page?''

"As ready as I'll ever be, I suppose." Page looked from him to Claire, then back to Elliot. "You were over here so long I wondered if Claire might be having a problem.''

"Nothing bad enough to prevent her from joining us,'' Elliot promised, his voice relaxed, cheerful. "Come on, you two, let's head out. Claire, your tent is near the path we'll be taking. Pick up your pack and stuff in a couple of candy bars and your canteen on the way out.''

He led them down through the trees and across a grassy meadow where colorful wildflowers of every description were scattered with a lavish hand. Soft pink shooting stars, dainty cranesbill geranium, brilliant yellow helianthella . . . and a multitude of other flowers with names none of the members had ever heard of were pointed out to them by Elliot. As they filed through another stand of pines he taught them to identify the various species by the variations in the bark, from the deeply grooved plates of the ponderosa to the smoother-scaled bark of the lodgepole pine. He pointed out a stand of the giant sequoias, allowing them a few minutes to enjoy their incredible size and then telling them to take a trip to Sequoia National Forest sometime to compare.

They finally halted the hike by a swift-moving creek running through a glade of white fir. All around them the Sierras reared in silent splendor, some of the higher peaks still covered with snow even at the end of June. Shrugging off packs and shoes and socks, the members relaxed and basked in the warmth of the sun, nibbling their candy and granola bars.

"You were absolutely right, Elliot,'' Donna lifted her arms and flung them wide. "This is incredible!''

"Stupendous!" chimed in Phil, flopping back into the tall meadow grass.

"Fantastic!" offered Doug, and everyone dissolved in laughter as they threw out more and more outrageous embellishments.

"Magnificent!"

"Resplendent!"

"It's okay," Rob yawned elaborately, and ducked when Brad threw a clump of grass at him.

Everyone picked up on the mood of rollicking gaiety and began playful wrestling matches and good-natured tussling. Claire had been sitting on one of the smooth boulders by the stream, smiling and relaxed even though she wasn't actually participating. Elliot was lying flat on his back, eyes closed and a grin on his face so that neither he nor Claire noticed Phil sneaking around behind the boulder. When he grabbed Claire from behind and completely swung her off her feet and into his arms, her reaction was instantaneous—and totally unexpected.

She screamed, limbs flailing as if her nightmare had come true. When an astounded Phil dropped her she turned on him like a doe at bay, eyes huge in a face stripped of all color. She held her arms up, poised to hold back an attack.

Exclamations of surprise and bewilderment rippled over the group, but Claire had no awareness of them. She was aware of nothing except the awful, choking fear—and the total humiliation of disgracing herself in such a manner. Her heart was pumping so wildly that her pulse throbbed in her ears, and she had no idea how long he had been talking when she finally heard Elliot's voice through the roar of her labored breathing.

"It's okay, honey. It's all right. No one is going to hurt you, Claire. Claire, look at me—it's Elliot, honey . . ." His voice was pitched low, so that it poured over her in a continuous flow of gentle words, coaxing her out of the wilderness of her fear.

With hesitant, trembling slowness she moved her head sideways until she saw Elliot and the deep gray pools of his eyes as they moved over her face. He was standing a few feet away, far enough not to intimidate, but close enough for her to reach out if she chose.

Behind him, frozen in uncertainty, was Phil, and the expression on his face would have been comical had Claire been in any condition to appreciate humor.

"I'm sorry," she tried to say, but the words emerged as a strangled croak. When Elliot took a step forward, his gaze steady but deeply lined, Claire could only stare in mute supplication. When he slowly, carefully held up his arms she found herself moving forward until they closed around her and she laid her head against his chest. Her hands clutched the front of his shirt so tightly the knuckles showed through whitely; she couldn't seem to stop trembling.

"Shh, you're okay now. Everything's okay . . ." Elliot kept up the soothing murmurs, bending his head so his mouth was right next to her ear. After a minute his hands began rubbing up and down her back in long, smooth strokes. Claire lay heavily against him, her body taut as the shivers continued to ripple through her.

Thank God she had at least allowed him to hold and comfort her! What in the name of heaven had happened to her?

"What happened?" Phil voiced Elliot's silent question, his voice almost cracking. "I was just cutting the fool—I didn't mean anything."

"Hey, man, you should have seen her when I offered to help with her tent," Michael started, subsiding abruptly when Elliot threw him a quelling look that would have stopped a charging grizzly.

Claire stirred, then lifted her head. She found Phil and tried to smile at him. "I'm sorry," she repeated, and this time, though still faint and quavery, the words were distinguishable.

She felt Elliot's hands move to her shoulders and gently tug until he could look down into her face. She met the compassion and determination with the same fatalistic calm that had anesthetized her last night, knowing she would have to break, at last, the long years of silence.

Everyone here deserved an explanation for her bizarre behavior, and Claire refused to be sucked back into the whirlpool of endless lies and pretense that had drowned her in its depths for a third of her life. Much easier to bear would be the horror, the pity, the humiliation she would endure for two weeks and then she would never have to see these people again. But what of Elliot? Her eyes closed.

"What, Claire? What is it, love?"

His voice was urgent, compelling, and only then did she realize she must have moaned his name aloud. With gallant grace she stepped back, out of the protective comfort of his embrace, her back straight, hands clasped in a death grip in front of her. Her head swiveled to encompass the entire group, and she took a long, tremulous breath that caught somewhere in her throat.

"I was married when I was just twenty-one," she spoke in an eerily calm voice devoid of expression. "My . . . husband . . . had a drinking problem." She tried again to take a deep breath, failed.

"He was, in fact, an alcoholic. Our . . . relationship was . . . not good, and—and I have some very bad memories that left a lot of scars." Her voice faltered now, and she didn't even notice that Elliot had moved closer and laid a hand upon her shoulder.

She didn't notice the expressions of sympathy and dawning understanding on everyone's faces, for she was lost in the agonizing catharsis that should have taken place long, long before now.

"We were married almost seven years before he—" her throat closed, and she struggled to finish,

121

"—before he died. I moved away, out here, started my business over . . . tried to make a new life. But—but I don't like—I mean whenever someone—"

"You don't have to explain anymore," Elliot interrupted very gently. "We understand, Claire."

Phil walked over a little closer, his boyish, lopsided face sheepish, the blue eyes regretful. "I'm sorry, Claire. If I'd had any idea I never would have grabbed you like I did."

Claire blinked rapidly. "I didn't want anyone to know," she whispered in a reed-thin voice.

"Why don't we take a walk?" Elliot suggested, nodding his head in silent thanks to Phil and indicating that he needed to move away. "I'm sure the others wouldn't mind entertaining themselves for a little while—would you prefer to have Josie or Bess go with you?"

Claire shook her head jerkily, avoiding Elliot's eyes as well as the speculative gazes of the others. She didn't want anyone else. She had to find out if Elliot had been repulsed by her pathetic, humiliating story; had to find out how he would treat her now that he knew some of her past. He must never, ever, though, learn all of her secrets. Somehow she must bury deeper the guilt, the shame, the way she had been reduced to a creature of hate as well as fear.

He led her along the creek and into the sheltering shadows of the trees, holding her hand in a light but firm clasp. They didn't speak until they were out of sight and sound of the rest of the group. There was nothing around them but the sound of the running water, for even the wind was still. Elliot led her over to a huge, sun-warmed boulder by the creek, its surface smooth from years of erosion. "Let's sit here," he said, waiting until Claire obeyed and then joining her. He sat close but without touching, though it took all his considerable self-control not to pull her into his arms.

Claire gazed up into the trees, not knowing what to say. She felt a queer, almost tingling numbness dulling her senses, as if she had been administered a shot of novocaine affecting her entire body. They would all be talking about her now, whispering and murmuring among themselves about her behavior, about the degrading story she had been forced to share.

Elliot was no doubt wishing he had insisted Josie or Bess come with her instead—he wouldn't even touch her now, or look her way. He had been repulsed by her revelation, contemptuous of her hysterical display. He would treat her with polite tolerance the rest of the time, and she was in love with him.

Without any warning a tiny sob burst from her lips, and Claire lifted her hand and pressed her fist against her mouth, turning her head away from Elliot. Not tears. She mustn't cry. That would be the straw that broke the camel's back, destroying the last tatters of her self-respect. The stubborn tears welled up behind her eyes anyway, aching for release and sliding unbidden down her cheeks when she refused to succumb to their demand. Another pitiful sob escaped.

"Ah, kitten . . . come here and cry it out."

Incredibly, unbelievably, she felt his hand close over her arm and tug, and his voice—he didn't sound repulsed or contemptuous at all. Still, it wouldn't do to give in to her feelings. She knew men hated tears, because every time her mom had ever cried her dad had gotten a hunted look on his face and left the house. Gary had ignored her the few times she had broken down in front of him, and then made snide remarks about how women always resorted to crying as their last weapon. And the only other time Elliot had seen her fighting tears he had been dismayed and appalled. So when his hand continued to urge her to turn around she resisted, shaking her head in a violent denial.

"Please don't turn away from me, Claire. There's no need to feel ashamed, you know. Let me comfort you as I want to do." His voice was tender, pleading and persuasive. When Claire did not stiffen in fear, only rejection, he slid over until their bodies were touching. "Turn around, lost lamb," he crooned in her ear. "I'm not going to force you, Claire. I want you to come to me because you want to, because you need me as much as I need for you to need me."

The words sank into her brain and she shifted around before she thought, her strained, red-rimmed eyes scanning Elliot's face in hope, in hunger, in disbelief.

"What?" she gasped out, the tears spurting afresh when Elliot nodded his head, affirming the words he had spoken. The dam burst, the barriers crumbled to dust as she crumpled into a weeping bundle, sobbing in his arms like a lost and frightened child.

Elliot let her cry it out, part of his heart hurting for her, but the larger part exulting in the knowledge that she did trust him enough now to turn to him of her own accord.

She's opened the door, Lord. Help me to show her Your love now. Help her to learn to trust in You as she is trusting in me.

Over her bowed head he stared into the distance, evaluating with clear-headed acceptance the burden he had shouldered. Claire was letting him closer, probably, than any other human being, perhaps including her own parents. If he took one wrong step, forced the pace one inch too fast, he could destroy her. She was already bruised from the past, and he knew she still hadn't fully shared all that had happened to her. God help him to never abuse this fragile trust and to continue to show him how to deal with the complicated, difficult, but potentially infinitely precious gem that was Claire Gerard.

The torrent eased at last, and Claire felt utterly

spent, yet somehow lightened. She had held all this inside for years, she realized, until it had encased her in armor so thick and heavy she had barely functioned as a human being. And she had not even been aware of it until Elliot Ramsey found the chink in that armor, steadily prying away until she lay bared before him. She stirred against the comforting arms, her throat raw, her chest tight. She had completely soaked his T-shirt, her hands were clutching him like a frightened koala cub, and she must look an absolute mess. What a nuisance she was!

"I'm sorry," she mumbled into his neck, her mouth brushing the warm tendons in his throat. He stiffened, and Claire reeled from the avalanche of sensation that toppled down onto her lacerated, hypersensitive emotions.

Moving in slow motion, his hand burrowed under her nape, fingers pressing as he gently forced her head back. His other hand lifted, wiping away the smudges of tears, the damp hair, with fingers that trembled. "Claire," he whispered hoarsely, "don't look at me like that. I can't stand it, and I'm only so strong when I'm this close to you."

Wonder filled her eyes, and her own fingers came up to hesitantly touch his lips, the strong contours of his jaw and chin. "You aren't repulsed," she breathed, the words throaty and filled with the same wonder in her eyes. "I cried all over you—made a fool of myself again—and you . . . you—"

Elliot's mouth stopped her observations and her arms slid around his shoulders in a convulsive embrace as they both gave in to the iridescent rainbow feelings arching over them in the aftermath of a storm of pent-up emotions.

CHAPTER 8

CLAIRE BATHED HER FACE in the icy water of the creek, using the crumpled handkerchief Elliot dug out of the hip pocket of his shorts. The shocking sting of the water helped to dispel the shyness which had overcome her when they had ended the passionate embrace. She had not dreamed she could respond with such abandonment to another man, and was just as incredulous that Elliot's heart was pounding, too. The dazed, smoldering look in his eyes caused the strangest sensation of satisfaction to twist her heart, and when she lifted her reddened, streaming face from the creek a captivating smile blossomed across her countenance.

Elliot grinned back ruefully. "Feeling pretty smug now, aren't you, Ms. Gerard? All you have to do is give me even a suggestion of a smile and I'm putty in your hands. And when we kiss—"

"Elliot!" she protested, blushing and holding the sopping handkerchief in front of her face.

"Are you ready to go back now?" he asked her after a minute in a very different tone, the blueness in his eyes changing to ambiguous blue-gray.

Claire sobered as well, though for some reason she found the thought of facing her nine trek mates less worrisome than she had such a short time ago. She gazed up at Elliot from where she was kneeling. "Your eyes change color as much as you say mine do," she told him and giggled at the absurdity of this observation.

The solemn cast of his face softened, and Elliot leaned over and hauled her to her feet, shaking his head. "Does that mean I'm now as easy to read as you are?"

Keeping her hands decorously on his chest, Claire sighed in contentment, ignoring the warning prick of her conscience telling her she would never read Elliot as he read her. "I doubt it," she murmured carelessly. "But right now I don't really mind as long as you keep reading me."

"Are you actually flirting with me now? What lovely femme fatale is rising from the ashes of her past, hmm?" Now, why had he gone and mentioned her past like a brainless idiot? He watched with a leaden feeling coating his insides as the light went out of her face and the smile withered and died.

"Kitten, don't. Don't let whatever monkeys that are still riding your back bring you down again. Claire, I—" he clamped his mouth shut so abruptly his jaw ached. Dear Lord, he had almost blurted it out loud to her, and at the worst possible time.

Okay, over to You. Get me out of this mess, Father, and give Claire back the joy of her salvation she felt so briefly before I loused it up. Humor. She had always responded to his offbeat humor. *Thanks, Lord.*

"I feel like you just pushed me into the creek, honey, and believe me, that's a cruel fate for anyone. Smile for me again, my sweet Claire, and don't freeze me out." He shuddered dramatically, wrapping his arms around her and mimicking a deep-throated 'burr-rr' in her ear. "Hold me close, darlin' . . . Don't put one of those monkeys on my back!"

It worked. She beat on him with gentle fists, the laughter bubbling up and melting the gathering ice floes of tension. "You're crazy . . . did you know that?"

"Crazy about you." He dropped a brief kiss on her upturned lips. "Come on now, let's go back. I know everyone's wanting to shower you with reassurance and caring and will complain that I'm trying to corner the market and monopolize you."

She was smiling when they came out of the glade and strolled back toward the group, and Elliot was holding her hand. Claire didn't care. She felt as if she were being allowed a brief moment of sunshine after years of dreary clouds and rain. She knew in the back of her head that all too soon she would lose to those clouds again, but for right now she grasped with both hands the marvelous, intoxicating feeling of release.

"Well, you certainly look like a different person, Claire," Donna announced as they rejoined the others. "What on earth did Elliot do to you, or do I need to ask?" She and Page looked at each other and giggled.

Josie looked at Donna reprovingly, then moved forward to give Claire a motherly hug. "I hope you are a different person, Claire, dear. You had been holding all that inside you far too long, I'll wager."

"My uncle's an alcoholic," Brad offered eagerly, his open eagerness to make her feel at ease touching her heart. "It's a bummer, isn't it?"

The awkward moment passed, and for the next several moments they all discussed the ramifications of drinking alcohol, until Elliot threatened to march them back double-time if they didn't pack it up. "We need to bathe in the hottest part of the day," he explained as everyone put socks and shoes and backpacks back on. "And I'm sure you'll all agree when I warn you that the water you'll be bathing in is every bit as cold as this creek here."

128

The discussion was successfully diverted and they discussed the rigors of wilderness bathing all the way back to camp. Claire stayed surprisingly relaxed, not even squirming inwardly when everyone took it for granted she would be hiking close to Elliot.

For the next several days Nature's Journeymen Trek IIB enjoyed idyllic conditions. The daily hikes were a welcome source of exercise and diversion, and the quiet moments of solitary introspection were times of renewal and cleansing. There had been a lot of joking about the cleansing of bodies, for as promised, Elliot had assigned them each a ten minute slot in which to bathe in the mountain pool on the far side of camp. Fed by streams of melting snow from the upper regions of the Sierras, it was every bit as frigid as Elliot had warned, and screams and squeals had echoed through the peaceful afternoon as each of the members was initiated.

Claire spent a lot of time reading her Bible, although she could not bring herself to join with the members who were sharing daily devotionals. Over and over she read the seventy-seventh Psalm, trying to grasp the enormity of it all. Her early Bible teaching had been lamentably sketchy, she acknowledged, and most of her memories were of stories about Daniel in the lion's den, Noah's ark, and Jesus with all the children on His lap. She had no idea of how to go about reading this Book, when her heart told her she had no right to claim its promises.

She had unburdened the load of the past, but she still carried the guilt, the shameful burden that she had grown to fear and despise her own husband, had wished him out of her life. It might even be her fault he was dead—it *was* her fault. She had no right to ask God to forgive her, after all, and no right to love Elliot. She had accepted the first long ago, but accepting the eventual renunciation of the man she had come to love with all her heart was no easy thing.

She started avoiding him in subtle ways, spending time with the Newman sisters, or on lonely walks around the camp and nearby hills. She spent a good portion of her time in her tent designing a house she had come to call her own dream design, for as she sketched and planned she knew she was dreaming that it was her house—and Elliot's.

Elliot himself helped her out, for it was as if he knew he had placed her in an awkward position the day of her confession, and was now striving to let her recover her balance and learn to be comfortable with the others. Every now and then Claire would find his eyes on her, however, searching her face with a deep, still concentration as if he were trying to take her apart and put her back together again. He never pried into her daily activities beyond asking if she were still reading her Bible, and Claire was grateful. She had no idea what she would do if he ever decided to probe her mind too intently about her relationship with God.

On the fourth day, when it was Claire's turn to bathe in the stream, she wandered down the path with heavy steps and a strange reluctance. She was depressed today. Depressed and aloof and withdrawn. The night before Phil and Page had taught them all how to play a silly game, and after endless prodding Claire had tried to join in.

She had been too stiff, too prudish, her partner Michael had finally told her. All she needed to do was relax, for crying out loud. Just because he wasn't Elliot Ramsey didn't mean he had the plague. Claire had crept off to her tent, telling Bess she was tired. Bess would have pursued the matter and even went to search out Elliot, who earlier had laughingly declined the proceedings for his nightly prowl about the far perimeters of the camp to make sure no wild animals were lurking about. She had either decided not to say anything—or Elliot had not wanted to bother with Claire—for he had not come to her tent.

Claire had slept very little, and the next morning hung back with Josie and Bess on the hike. Even then Elliot had not openly sought her out or questioned her evasion, leaving Claire with the dismal conclusion that it was all over between them. As she swiftly shed her clothes she reminded herself through clenched teeth that there was actually nothing to "be over between them" in the first place. With a grim shudder she plunged into the pool as was her custom. Trying to slide in slowly, an inch at a time, had ended up with her not taking a bath at all the first day.

The shock of the icy water was diverting enough to allow her to forget her misery for a moment. She hurriedly washed with the biodegradable soap provided by Nature's Journeymen, goose pimples covering her body in spite of the vigorous scrubbing. She was just about to scramble out when her eye caught on something so amazing she froze where she was sitting, mouth dropping open in disbelief.

Across the pool, along the shallow edge, a small, fat little bird was burying his head in the water like a duck. But this wasn't a duck; the beak, the feet, the smooth gray shape was most definitely a bird's shape. After a few minutes, with a shake of its little head and ruffling of feathers, this—this ridiculous creature fluttered nearer the center of the pool, dived, and completely disappeared. Claire did not notice how cold her body had become, or that she had turned a dangerous shade of blue about her extremities. She watched in open-mouthed fascination as the bird reappeared with a smug expression on its face, swallowed something, and then disappeared beneath the water once more.

Only after she inadvertently sneezed and the bird flew off with a lovely trilling scold directed across the stream at her did Claire realize with a start that she was going to be late. Elliot was very strict about bathing, for the dangers of hypothermia were very real, even in the height of summer. She found she couldn't grasp her towel, and dried off half-heartedly. For some reason she was sleepy, and it didn't seem that important to dry off totally anyway. Eventually she managed to drag on her clothes, and was fumbling indifferently with shoestrings when she heard her name called.

"I was sent to make sure you hadn't turned into a frozen mermaid," Page greeted her with a sunny smile. "You've been gone longer than you're supposed to be, our intrepid leader informed me, and would I please come and fetch you."

Claire stood slowly, her whole body feeling sluggish. Why on earth was she so sleepy? "Thanks. I'm fine."

Page looked at her strangely. "You look a little funny."

Funny. What was it she had seen that was so funny? "I saw this bird," she began, noting that Page was still looking at her in a peculiar way. "It kept disappearing under the water, like a duck. But it was a bird." She giggled, stumbled, then shivered as a breeze playfully whistled through her damp clothes.

"Are you all right, Claire?" Page turned to stare as they walked up through the trees.

"I'm a little cold, still," Claire offered. "I think I prefer hot showers." Even to her own less than alert ears the words sounded heavy and slurred. No wonder Page was looking at her like she was . . . was that ridiculously funny little bird.

"Yeah . . . what I wouldn't give for my tub right now." Page glanced around as they entered the camp site. "Well, if you're sure you're okay I'm going to go on the hike with the others." She slanted a veiled look at Claire. "You sure you don't want to come? Elliot wasn't real pleased when you declined, you know."

Claire shook her head. All she wanted to do right now was sleep. "Going to take a nap," she mumbled, not seeing Page's relieved look.

"I'll tell him. See you later."

It seemed like moments—or was it hours—later when she heard a voice calling her name insistently. Claire lay huddled inside her sleeping bag, where she had crawled to try and get warm. Time had ceased to be an orderly progression of seconds and minutes, for all she knew was she was so miserably cold she wanted to die. It was usually hot in her tent in the afternoons. What was the matter with her?

CHAPTER 9

"CLAIRE!" THE VOICE CALLED AGAIN. "Answer me, Claire, or I'm coming in."

Claire tried to reply. She even tried to sit up, but her limbs refused to obey and she rolled over with a sigh, her body shuddering and shaking. There was the sound of the zipper and then hands were touching her, feeling her head, her arms, and from somewhere above her she thought she heard a man's voice. Was it Elliot's?

No. He didn't care about her anymore. Besides, he was put out with her and had taken the others on a hike. When the hands firmly rolled her onto her back she didn't resist, barely forcing herself to open heavy-lidded eyes. Oh. It was Elliot. He was frowning. Was he that angry with her? Oh, well, what did it matter? Nothing mattered anymore, because she was simply too tired and cold to care.

"Claire! Keep your eyes open—don't go to sleep." Warm hands surrounded her face, and she sighed pleasurably, turning her cheek into the warmth.

"Claire!" the voice repeated, the tone urgent now,

commanding. "Talk to me—what happened to you? Why did you stay in the water too long? You little idiot! You're on the verge of hypothermia, and if you don't help me I'm going to have to radio for a chopper. Claire!" She was suddenly being shaken, and she opened her mouth to protest.

Elliot had experienced fear before, but not in the concentrated dose he was experiencing now. *God in heaven*, he prayed desperately, *help me to warm her up. Please, God. Please.*

He left Claire's side long enough to stick his head out the door. "Doug! Josie! Get over here now!" When they came running over he didn't waste time or words.

"Claire is on the verge of hypothermia. If we don't get her body temperature up I'll have to air evac her out. Doug, I need you to build a fire and ask some of the others to gather some large, smooth stones. Josie, I need for you to get Claire out of her clothes and zipped back in her sleeping bag. Let me know the minute you've done that."

Claire feebly protested this invasion, stilling only when Josie promised her over and over that she would be warmer if she took off her damp clothes. Someone held her up while someone else held a cup to her lips and forced Claire to swallow untold amounts of hot liquid. Where was Elliot?

"I'm right here, love. Come on, keep fighting it, Claire. You've got to fight it."

"She'll be okay, Elliot. We're all praying for her."

"That may be so, but God isn't going to suspend the laws of nature every time some innocent fool breaks them."

"Where did you want these hot stones, Elliot? We've wrapped them in towels like you told us."

"Put that one at her feet—here . . . those on either side . . . that's it."

Oh, that blessed warmth! Claire felt it seeping back

into her bones, felt the awful, clammy, chilling cold gradually fading away. She wanted to talk to Elliot, ask him if that had been his voice sounding so agonized. Or was it Josie's? She had finally recognized the woman, and was sorry for the look of deep concern lining her face. It was her fault. She was guilty—guilty—guilty—

"Claire, it's all right. Don't talk like that. The last thing you need is to tote around a sackload of guilt."

When she finally came fully to herself once more the first thing Claire noticed was how hot and tired Elliot looked. Why, he was covered with sweat! Her hand lifted in wonder and traced lightly down Elliot's dripping arm.

"You're covered with perspiration," she announced in a wisp of a voice that nonetheless caused him to snap around and stare down at her in relief. Her eyes wide and wondering, she watched as Elliot's head dropped between his hands.

"Thank you, Lord," he murmured, his voice catching. "Oh, thank you, Lord!"

"Elliot?" she whispered uncertainly.

He lifted his head, picked up her hand, and smiled. "When you've regained your strength I plan to discipline you thoroughly, Ms. Claire Gerard." He glanced around. "And a few other members of this trek plan to help me out."

Claire looked around her crowded tent, which at the moment looked like it was about to burst at the seams. Josie was on her other side, and behind Elliot she saw Doug's bearded face. She colored faintly, and tried to smile back at Elliot.

"I think I've made a fool of myself again, haven't I?" she asked in resignation, too weary to feel much embarrassment. Her mind worked back over the recent past, coming to rest on the fact that she was finally no longer suffering from the enervating, aching cold.

"I got too cold, didn't I?" She kept her eyes fastened on Elliot, who nodded grimly.

"You were very lucky, my sweet accident-looking-for-a-place-to-happen." His fingers reached and felt her brow, her cheeks, then he lifted her wrist to take her pulse. "My biggest challenge in the history of Nature's Journeymen, I think, is going to be getting you out of the Sierras in one piece."

"Thanks." Her lashes fell, then swept upward again as she remembered all that had happened. "Oh, Elliot, I truly didn't do it on purpose, but I saw this bird. It was a bird, too, only it was acting like a duck, or a pelican—or a seagull. But it was so tiny—I just couldn't believe it!"

"A water ouzel." Elliot's stern demeanor relaxed, and he touched her nose gently. "I can understand, even if you did scare us all half to death." He glanced over at Josie, and then behind to Doug. "The water ouzel is one of nature's clowns. It's a member of the thrush family, but I think if the ouzel had its way it would have been a fish because it loves water so much. What Claire was privileged enough to see is quite true—the bird will actually walk along the bottom of a pool searching for bugs." He grinned down at Claire. "I wish I'd been there, although I'm afraid if I had, my mind wouldn't have been on the bird."

"Elliot!" Claire gasped, and Doug roared with laughter.

"I think her temperature has definitely soared now, Elliot," he chuckled, winking at Claire. "I'll go spread the good news to the others."

"I think I better help Claire dress," Josie observed in a very dry voice.

Elliot kept Claire trapped within the tender depths of his gaze. "You're right, Josie," he agreed without looking at the older woman. "But first, I need to do two things." He held out one hand to Josie, clasping

137

Claire's with his other. Then he bowed his head and closed his eyes.

"Most gracious and loving Father," he prayed in a deep voice that sent an entirely different set of chills cascading down Claire's spine, "I thank You for restoring Claire to our midst without undue harm, and pray that You will watch over her in a special way. She needs watching over, Lord, and I am so grateful for Your eyes which never sleep, and Your hands which are always open for us to reach out."

There was a little silence when he closed his prayer, then Claire cleared her throat. "You said there were two things," she said to avoid her reaction to his prayer, a question in her voice and eyes.

Within the dim confines of the tent Elliot's eyes seemed to catch fire and burn with a flame of shooting silver. "That's right, I did," he murmured. His gaze flicked up to Josie and he grinned.

"With your permission, ma'am . . ."

Josie's grin matched his own, but Claire only looked bewildered, watching in rosy confusion as Elliot lowered his head to hers. He kissed her mouth once, twice, then moved away. "Josie can help you dress now. I'll see you in a little while."

"You better try to be more careful," Josie scolded her as she helped her put on fresh clothes. "Not only for your health, but ours as well."

"I know I've been a nuisance," Claire began, her voice awkward, but Josie shushed her.

"You could never be a nuisance, my dear," she promised her gently. "I mean something entirely different, although I have my doubts as to whether I ought to mention it or not."

There was a twinkle in her eye and laughter in the words, but Claire was uneasy. "What on earth do you mean, Josie?"

"Our group leader, honey. One Elliot Ramsey. If you don't take better care of yourself I'm afraid Elliot is going to collapse from worry, and then all eleven of us will perish out here in the wilderness."

"I don't know what you mean. Elliot doesn't care about me that much." She kept her face averted.

"Child, the man is head over heels in love with you. Just as you are with him." Josie sank back on her heels and regarded Claire in exasperation. "Why on earth the two of you don't quit pretending is beyond me. Do you think the rest of us are blind?"

"He doesn't love me. He can't." Claire's voice was agonized, almost breaking, and Josie drew her against her ample shoulder.

"And why on earth shouldn't he be in love with you? You're a lovely woman and any man would be lucky to have you."

Claire shook her head. "No. No man would be lucky, and I don't have the right, anyway." She backed away from Josie and began rummaging in her pack for her brush with blind fingers. "I don't have the right," she repeated.

Josie gazed at her intently, opened her mouth, and then shut it again. After a minute, when Claire kept her back to her and just brushed her hair over and over, Josie patted her shoulder and unzipped the flap. "I'll leave you alone, dear. But I want you to think about what I said."

For the rest of the week Claire was teased continually about her close brush with hypothermia, and the fact that she was turning into the camp albatross. The others might have blistered feet, skinned knees, and Donna a case of sunburn, but the favorite phrase among the members became "Watch out, wilderness, here comes Claire!"

The relentless bantering about her mishaps finally succeeding in relaxing Claire's guard, although she still felt awkward around Elliot after Josie's pronouncement. What was it about the lovers being the last to know? Elliot continued to treat her with circumspection, though he now refused to allow her to keep to herself except for private devotionals. She participated in every hike, stayed with the group for evening sing-alongs and sharing, and even when she made her way to the privy stationed some distance away behind a shield of evergreens Claire knew he was aware of it.

In a paradoxical sort of way this encompassing show of caring caused her to relax outwardly, while still withdrawing inside. The men were all solicitous, but always careful not to "invade her space," as Brad put it. The younger women shared their own men problems, and Page promised to show her different ways to wear her rebellious curls when they returned to civilization. The Newman sisters chatted about their various students, and the rambling old house they had inherited from their father. "Maybe we ought to hire you and Elliot to refurbish it," Bess had gushed one time, earning a pained look from Claire and a sharp elbow from Josie.

Claire found, however, that her thoughts were shifting more and more to introspection and soul searching. Elliot had been right. Out here it was so much easier to be still and know God, even if in the past the only God she had known had been a terrifying God of judgment. She read "her" psalm at least once a day, wondering what had happened to the psalmist and if it could possibly be worse than what she had done. And yet . . . and yet not one of these strangers who were rapidly turning into friends had ever condemned her for being married to an alcoholic. Phil had shared his own problems with drinking just to be part of some gang, and how he had overcome it through the love of Christ and other caring friends. If God could forgive Phil, could he forgive her, too? Claire had wanted to ask so badly the words crowded up in her throat and choked her. But she hadn't. Maybe if she had been alone with Elliot . . .

She must stop such forbidden thoughts. What if God chose to punish her by having something awful happen to Elliot? She might have never prayed for anything bad to happen to Gary, but begging God to keep him away from her, secretly hoping that somehow, someday Gary would decide not to come home—wasn't that about the same? And if she continued to pine for Elliot she might end up causing a similar fate to befall him. And yet . . . and yet when they were hiking across sunlit meadows and stopped to inspect the dainty, fragile pink petals of a shooting star it was somehow difficult to imagine God as the Supreme Being holding a big club and striking at some unknown moment. And when Elliot pointed out a tiny alpine chipmunk perched on a rotting log eating his noon meal, completely oblivious to his captivated audience, it was almost easy to imagine a loving Supreme Being who truly did care when a sparrow fell.

At times like those Claire wanted to be close to God. She wanted Elliot's faith, or even Phil's serene confidence that he had been forgiven. If she tried to talk to, well, to Jesus as she had talked to Elliot would it make a difference? Could she really have a relationship with her Savior? It was one thing to have accepted years ago that Christ had died for her, and because of His willingness to do so she would eventually go to heaven. It was something else altogether, after almost a decade of fear and trembling, to consider that, as a Christian, she could have an entirely different kind of life.

"You're looking mighty pensive." Elliot dropped down beside her without warning, and Claire was unable to quell the momentary shrinking.

She had just finished rinsing out her dishes after supper and was sitting in front of her tent, lost in thought. She saw immediately that she had hurt Elliot by her involuntary withdrawal, and without thinking reached out her hand and touched his arm.

"I truly didn't mean to do that," she promised him, searching his face earnestly. "I'm not afraid of you anymore, Elliot. Really, I'm not. I—I still seem to startle easily, though."

He relaxed, his hand coming to cover hers and squeezing briefly. "I'm glad. After all we've been through in the last week it would have been hard to accept if you still felt nervous around me." He looked down at her with an intense directness he had not shown in a long time. "You still go out of your way to avoid me, though. Can you tell me why, if it's not because you're afraid of me?"

Claire hoped the late evening shadows hid the scalding blush that moved up her throat and covered her cheeks. "I didn't want to give everyone more room to talk—they consider us enough of an . . . item . . . as it is."

"So they do." He stretched his legs and leaned back on his elbows, and grinned at her. With his ruffled black hair, tanned face, and those light, piercing eyes he presented a devastating picture of vibrant, confident masculinity. Claire gaped at him helplessly.

"Doesn't bother me in the slightest," he continued in a sunny, careless tone, "although I have noticed a few black looks in your direction by Page. Actually," he was looking up into the branches of the pines now, "I'm sort of glad we've been paired off because it keeps her off my back. For some strange reason she seems to think I'd be a good prospect for a romantic fling. I can't understand it—can you?" He looked back at Claire, twin devils dancing in his eyes.

Claire collapsed in giggles, the aura of sadness and loneliness evaporating like morning mist.

"You . . . are . . . impossible!" she gasped out at last, shaking her head as her heart bubbled and frothed over with love. Never, ever had she known anyone who could make her laugh like this, make her forget for blissful spans of time who she was and what she was.

If there was any mercy this side of heaven, surely God would allow her to bask in this love for a short while. She would never ask for more than that. Just to hold this moment to her, when Elliot was gazing at her with teasing affection, and she could smile back in joy—just for this moment.

CHAPTER 10

SUMMER THUNDERSTORMS IN THIS SECTION of the Sierras were rare, but late that Saturday night one descended upon Nature's Journeymen Trek IIB. A resounding clap of thunder was followed by a deluge of driving rain that rendered seeing beyond one's nose impossible. The wind howled, the trees swayed, and through the furor Elliot made his way from tent to tent, checking on his awed and apprehensive charges. He reassured each one that as long as they stayed inside they would remain safe and dry, that the storm would blow over before long, and in the morning they would wonder if it had all been a bad dream.

Because Claire had set her tent up so far apart from the others, she was the last person Elliot checked. He made his way across the site bent almost double against the driving wind and cold, stinging downpour, not realizing until he was practically on top of Claire's tent that he should have checked her first. A quick, incredulous sweep of the flashlight revealed a crumpled mass of nylon with poles flapping wildly about. From within the collapsed tent a moving, billowing lump was having little luck fighting both natural and man-made elements.

Without wasting time on speculations Elliot pawed through the folds and found the zipper fastening to the front flap. "Claire!" he shouted above the storm. "Just be still! I'll have you out in a minute!" It was difficult to work in the darkness. The erratic light cast by his flashlight stuck beam upwards in the wet ground was too feeble to help much, and the lashing rain hampered his fingers while the wind tugged at the writhing nylon. He was successful eventually, working the flap open enough to drag Claire out. She had at least managed to pull the zipperless plastic poncho over her head, but it was on backwards, and one sleeve hung limp and empty. Elliot felt his lips twitch.

"Don't you dare say *one* word!" Claire threatened in a muffled voice. "Not one word!" She twisted her head, trying to wipe her face free of her hair, the rain, and dripping poncho so that she could see.

Elliot did not waste time. He picked up the flashlight and thrust it in Claire's free hand, bent, picked her up twisted poncho and all, then slowly maneuvered back between the trees over to his own tent. Inside, he deposited his dripping bundle in one corner, then tugged the poncho over her head. Claire glared at him in a wavering yellow circle cast by his flashlight, her hair a riotous mass of dampened honey-toned curls and her body clad in the T-shirt he had given her—on top of her own long-sleeved, high-necked, lace-edge nightie. Elliot couldn't help it. Convulsed with whooping gasps of laughter, he turned away from her to tug off his own rain-slick cagoule, dropping it on top of her poncho.

The rain pattered in a drumming tattoo against the walls of his tent, and the wind whistled and beat at the flexible, resistant sides. Although Elliot's tent was large enough for three people, the air in the roomier space inside rapidly grew steamy, clammy, and rife with pungent odors of plastic, rain . . . and Elliot.

Claire stayed where she was, her head just touching the roof, arms clutching her sides, and her eyes spitting mad. How dare he laugh at her like this, as if she were some fumbling klutz who didn't know better than to knock her tent down around her while struggling to pull on a stupid plastic poncho . . . and then practically suffocating before being rescued?

Except that was exactly what she was. Elliot's howls and shaking shoulders, added to the ludicrous picture she must make, were too much for Claire. Frustration, embarrassment, twinges of fear all swirled away as laughter overcame her as well. She sank to her knees, laughing until tears streamed down her cheeks, and suddenly she knew she wasn't laughing at all. Burying her face in her hands, crouched in the corner of Elliot's blessedly secure tent, she struggled feebly against the emotional storm rampaging through her. All she had done since she came up in the mountains was cry. What a useless, irritating female he must think she was! How inept, awkward, and totally incompetent as well.

"Claire . . . honey . . . are you crying?" He touched her shoulder, his voice still fighting the laughter even as he posed the question.

"Now why should I have anything to cry about?" Claire sobbed in teary sarcasm. "My tent is ruined, I look like a freak in a sideshow, and—and all I've done since I met you is make a great big colossal fool of myself!"

With easy strength he hauled her into his arms and shimmied both of them across and on top of his sleeping bag. Holding her in his lap as if she were a child, he brushed gentle hands down her back, across her shoulders, and pushed stray locks of hair out of her face. "You haven't made a fool of yourself, little one," he soothed tenderly, his lips brushing her temple in a soft caress. "You're just out of your element up here, and on top of that you're having to face things you've avoided facing for years. Both your body and your emotions have been battered pretty relentlessly. It's no wonder you've probably shed as many tears as the raindrops in this storm."

"Don't tease me right now, Elliot," she choked. "Please."

"All right . . . all right." He laid his cheek against her head and said no more, merely holding her close while she sniffed and shook.

"Do a lot of women cry all over you?" she ventured after awhile in a hoarse, hesitant voice. She tried to free herself, but desisted when Elliot tightened his arms.

"I do think you hold the record," he informed her, the hint of a smile back in his voice. "But I don't mind, Claire." His voice went soft and smoky. "In fact, I'm glad."

"You're gl—glad?" Claire lifted her head, tried to search his features in the inky darkness.

"Very glad," he repeated, and dropped a kiss on her upturned nose. "The Claire Gerard I met so many months ago would never have dreamed of showing her emotions like you have up here, much less allowed me to get close enough to give her comfort. So you see, I have a lot to be glad about. You cry on my shoulder anytime you want, Claire Gerard."

"My husband always said women used tears as a weapon," Claire found herself confessing. "He—he used to get so angry I just stopped crying in front of him, in front of anybody."

"Some women might do that." Elliot shifted slightly, but kept his arms firmly around Claire. "In fact, my sister used to try it on occasion when we were growing up."

"I didn't know you had a sister."

"She's a model down in L.A. now." His voice was sad. "She rebelled against everything and everyone when she was fifteen—turned her back on God completely. It just about broke my parents' hearts. They disapprove of her lifestyle, but they know they can't tell her how she should live her life anymore. But they still pray for her every day, and I do, too." He hesitated, then added softly, "Just as I pray for you every day, Claire."

Claire felt her heart give a gigantic leap of love before she remembered Elliot's prayers on her behalf would have to go unheeded.

"It won't do any good," she sighed against his shoulder, unconsciously snuggling closer to drive away the demons of guilt and despair.

Elliot went very still. "And why not?" He reached over suddenly and picked up his gas lantern. In spite of working around Claire's recumbent body, with the ease of years' worth of experience he struck a match and lit it so that a larger pool of light showed her face more clearly. "Why won't praying for you do any good, Claire?"

Claire tried to hide her face, not wanting to be exposed. "Couldn't you turn off the lantern?" she pleaded into the warm softness of his T-shirt.

Elliot forced her to look up into his face, his eyes shadowed and deep, but still full of awesome perceptiveness. "The Bible tells us God is light, and that there is no darkness in Him at all. Stop trying to hide from me—and from Him—in the darkness, Claire. Tell me now, where we can see each other in the light, why you feel you're beyond redemption?"

She stiffened, wanting to struggle, wanting to yank herself free and flee into the—into the darkness. But part of her, the part newly awakened in the past week to the urgent need for love, for light, for reconciliation, responded to Elliot's demand. She heard herself uttering aloud the words she had carried in her heart for so many years, the words condemning her forever to a life of penance and guilt.

"I was—when Gary died—I was *relieved*, Elliot.

Part of me was even glad. I never prayed for him to die—I knew that was wrong—but I wasn't sorry. I had grown to . . . to hate him as much as I was afraid."

She didn't realize she was clutching him with such blind force that his shirt was in danger of tearing until Elliot gently pried loose her hands. Even then she didn't react, too lost in the painful outpouring of her dreaded secret burden.

"I couldn't tell anyone. They all thought Gary was a good old boy, a caring, jolly-go-lucky man who just enjoyed the good life. He was so careful, you see, to always present a good front to my parents, my friends, the church . . . and for a long time I wanted to protect him, and try to help him change."

Her voice went flat, a dull lifeless monotone that only emphasized the depth of feeling. "I had promised to love and honor him in front of God and man, and when the love turned to . . . hate and fear, and the honor turned to contempt, I felt I had violated God's laws as well as my marriage vows." She twisted, looking straight up into his face with beseeching, tortured eyes. "I don't *deserve* your prayers, Elliot, because even if I didn't pull out a gun and shoot him, I'm guilty of my husband's death just the same. It was my fault—I should have handled him differently, should have prayed for strength instead of praying he would go away and never return."

"How did your husband die?"

"Car crash. What else?" Her voice was bleak. "He was drunk, of course, and had just finished—" she stopped.

Elliot waited, not saying a word or moving beyond tightening the arms holding her so closely.

"I–I didn't even try to stop him. At the time I didn't care where he was going or for how long, as long as it was away from me." She shook her head from side to side, a wounded animal seeking shelter that wasn't there. "I didn't care. I didn't ever want to see him again."

She closed her eyes, missing the wealth of compassion in Elliot's face. "I was so filled with fear, with hatred, that I didn't care. So he died, and I'll spend the rest of my life regretting that I didn't try to stop him."

"*Could* you have stopped him, Claire?" He held her chin in a firm grip, and his voice was calm, neutral. "Think about it and tell me if I'm wrong. You weren't in any condition yourself to be able to have physically stopped him, were you?"

"I still should have tried. He was drunk, out of his head. He didn't know—"

"Did you put the drinks in his hand that caused him to become drunk?" Still the same calm, neutral tone and the unswerving directness of gaze. He wasn't going to let her hide anymore.

"No! I wouldn't let him bring any of it in the house—or at least I tried. He was good at hiding it."

Elliot took her by the shoulders then, turning her around so she was directly in front of him. "Then who was responsible, my love? You didn't cause him to become drunk, and you were physically incapable of stopping him from leaving. I repeat, who was responsible?"

Claire gazed back at him hopelessly. "I know in my head that it was Gary's fault, but I can't seem to get the message to my heart. He was sick, but I was too young and too ignorant—too naive to understand until it was too late. And when I could have used my Christian faith to help—I used it to destroy instead. God doesn't have anything else to give me but judgment, Elliot."

She sagged suddenly, her voice dying away. "I feel so tired. Do you think you could help me fix my tent?" She stirred, forced her drooping lids up, "I'm sorry, Elliot. This can't have been pleasant for you. I'll be all right in the morning . . .

150

"Shh, shh, rest easy, little one. You're going to have to stay here, but I don't want you to be afraid."

"I'm not. I love you." With a last sigh of infinite weariness she curled up into his arms again, consciousness slipping away as her body overrode her mind. Too much had happened too quickly, and sleep was a necessary safety valve to avoid breaking down completely.

Elliot held her until her breathing was deep and even, and the hands clutching him relaxed and slid limply to her lap. His eyes were damp with tears of bitter compassion—and incredulous joy. She had verbalized her love for him! She might be completely worn down emotionally, and would doubtless feel awkward if not downright withdrawn come morning, but she had told him she loved him.

Thank You, Lord. Thank You. With exquisite care he eased her away from his body and down into his sleeping bag, leaning to touch his lips to her brow.

"Sleep, my tormented lamb," he breathed silently. "Rest and be healed. In the morning your sorrowful song will, I pray, turn into one of joy."

Father, I love her. I love her more than I ever thought it was possible to love another human being. But she's still too afraid of You, still too bound by her guilt for me to ask her to be my wife. Help me. Show her Your love, Your compassion and forgiveness. Please, Lord—

A wavering light reflected dimly off the walls, and a soft voice full of apprehension called his name. "Elliot? Are you in there?"

He moved swiftly to the doorway, noting with absent shock that the storm had blown over. Josie and Bess were confronting him, and he gave a rueful smile.

"We went to check on Claire now that the rain has stopped," Josie spoke rapidly, her voice worried. "Elliot, her tent—"

151

"She's fine, Josie," Elliot interrupted. "I've got her in here with me. She's asleep."

"Oh, dear, do you think that's wise, Elliot?" Bess asked. "I'm sure you're a gentleman, but I still don't think—I mean what will the others think—"

"Do be quiet, Bessie!" Josephine admonished her sister, waving the flashlight irritably. "What Elliot and Claire do is none of our business, although I do not for one minute think either of them would do anything shameful or immoral."

"Thanks for the vote of confidence," Elliot inserted dryly. He took their flashlight, flicked it off, then held up the tent flap.

"Here," he whispered. "See for yourself. She's exhausted or I would have resurrected her tent and let her go back. But I'm not going to wake her up now."

The sisters pondered Claire's slumbering form silently a minute, then backed out of the tent. Elliot gave the flashlight back to Josie, who switched it back on.

"You will be careful with her, Elliot," she ventured reluctantly, as if she knew the warning was unnecessary but felt compelled to make it anyway. "She strikes me as a particularly vulnerable, sensitive woman."

"You don't need to worry." The quiet conviction in his voice rang out in the cool, crystalline clear stillness of the rain-washed night. "I'd cut off my arm before I'd hurt her, or allow anyone else to."

Josie touched his arm. "We know, Elliot." She turned to Bess then and gestured toward their tents. "Come on, sister, let's get back inside where it's warm."

"We'll help any way we can," she tossed over her shoulder, the calm promise floating back from the darkness.

Elliot went back into his tent, unearthed a thin cotton blanket, and spent the rest of the night until dawn keeping a loving vigil over the woman sleeping unknowing beside him.

Claire woke slowly, stretching her body and wondering sleepily why she felt as if she had just finished a ten-mile hike with a thirty-pound pack. She turned her head, and was shocked into instant wakefulness by the sight of Elliot sitting beside her. His knees were drawn up to his chest and his chin was resting on his hands.

Memories assaulted her from all sides until with a groan she slid farther down and pulled the sleeping bag over her head. "Oh, what a mess!" she wailed, the cry muffled beneath the cushiony layers of down.

Elliot chuckled and swiped the cover back. "Hiding won't do any good," he chided her with a grin. "You might as well come on out and face the music. I've brought you some clothes so at least you won't have to tiptoe through the trees while an audience of nine applauds you on."

"Oh—hh! Can't I just spend the next week in here? You can have my tent, and I'll come out after dark like the skunks and raccoons and eat . . ."

"Claire." He cut across her gently, "You're babbling, honey."

Claire had drawn up her knees like Elliot and now hid her face between them. "I know," she told the knees because she couldn't tell Elliot. "It's easier than facing you after what happened last night."

"What are you having the most trouble with—telling me about your husband, or telling me you love me?" He moved until he was able to reach and lay one hand on her shoulder.

Hectic color swarmed over her face and throat. "Both!" she mumbled, wondering if she could ever recover her poise again. "Not to mention my tent . . ."

"You did look pretty comical. Sort of like an old 'I

153

Love Lucy' rerun.'' When she groaned and tried to turn away he stopped her by pulling her into his lap the way he had the night before. "Claire . . . you don't have to be embarrassed,'' he murmured with great tenderness in her ear. "I love you, too, you see.''

Frozen with shock, she lifted her head and gaped at him. "But you can't,'' she denied in a strangulated voice. "You can't love me.''

Elliot began combing his fingers through her wildly disordered hair. "And why not?'' he asked calmly.

His calmness helped, and she relaxed within his hold, telling him with defeated passivity, "Because I don't deserve to have any man's love, especially a man like you. And because I know something horrible would happen to you if I accepted your love and tried to give you mine.''

He had expected something like this, but he had not anticipated the depth of his own pain and frustration, or how hard it was to completely subdue it. "Are you saying you feel God will punish you for loving me by causing something bad to happen—to me?'' He took her face between her hands, reading the naked misery there and feeling as if he were facing a black, bottomless chasm.

"Claire, that isn't true. God loves you—He forgave you for all the feelings you had for your husband long ago. All you have to do is accept it, and grow in His love. In our love.''

"The Bible says 'Vengeance is mine, I will repay.' '' She swallowed hard. "I've been searching and hoping ever since I started reading the Bible you gave me, Elliot. I want the kind of relationship with Jesus you have, that Phil and the Newman sisters and Rob have. I—I've even tried praying like I used to do, but there's nothing. Nothing.'' She put her hands over Elliot's and drew them down, placing frantic little kisses all over them before holding them tightly.

"Then I found this verse in Isaiah—it warns that our iniquities separate us from God, and that He won't hear us because He has hidden His face. It even talks about hands being stained with blood, 'your fingers with guilt.'" She quoted the verse with a kind of pathetic vehemence that tore Elliot's heart. "That's me. I'm guilty, and I can never atone for it—never. I know Jesus died for my sins and when I die I'll go to heaven, but it doesn't keep me from being guilty."

For a long moment Elliot did not speak. He prayed desperately, as he had never before prayed, knowing if he couldn't fight through to her soon he would lose forever the woman he loved more than he loved himself. *You know I can't do it, Lord. Only through Your Spirit, by Your power, can she ever understand. Oh, God, please answer her song in the night!*

"Let's not talk about it anymore right now, okay? After you eat and clean up and have a chance to see things in perspective maybe we can talk again." He drew her to her feet. "But I want you to promise me you'll keep one thing uppermost in your mind."

"What?" She quivered within his embrace, wanting him to hold her forever, dreading the separation she would have to force upon them.

"This," he ground out roughly, and kissed her with all the pent-up passion he had carefully guarded for so long. He drew her arms around his neck, forcing her response with a loving persuasion Claire could not fight. When he felt her melt against him, her arms tightening about his neck, he gently pulled away. Holding her at arms' length, he captured her dazed, drugged eyes and held them with the sheer force of his willpower.

"I love you," Elliot stated flatly. "And you love me. Nothing can change that, or the way we respond to one another, and as God as my witness I won't give up until you're mine."

As if they all knew she was suffering more than the ignominy of a collapsed tent, the other members of the trek refrained from teasing Claire overmuch, although there was enough gentle ribbing to try and make her feel less humiliated. When she had finally joined everyone at breakfast, Michael and Page started to make suggestive comments about her spending the night in Elliot's tent, but Elliot had only needed to direct one chilling glare in their direction.

"I do my best to live my faith so I can proclaim it without shame," he had told them with steely intent. "Do *not* make the mistake of spreading gossip or innuendo about what happened last night—because nothing did. Do I make myself clear?"

Claire remembered what Boyd had said about Elliot's ability to instill the fear of God with a glance, and had smiled at the way both Michael and Page had avoided her for the rest of the day. Elliot had helped her re-pitch her tent, joking with Doug and Phil as they worked, treating Claire with an easy familiarity designed to keep her relaxed. She went for a walk with Josie and Bess after lunch, took a nap, and was almost in control of her turbulent emotions when Elliot stopped by.

"Give me your Bible," he ordered her, smiling a little as she obeyed without question. "I want to mark some passages for you to read before we go on our night hike this evening. Will you promise to try and read with an open mind?"

She looked at him, her heart in her eyes, her mouth tightened against the pain. "I'll try, Elliot, but please don't expect too much."

"I don't," he returned quietly. "I expect it all."

After he left Claire wandered a little ways into the stand of trees beyond her tent to a small patch of sunlit grass she had found. Hands trembling, she opened the Bible to 1 John, the first chapter Elliot had marked; finding a short note on the marker. "I quoted from this chapter last night," it read, "and now I want you to read the ninth verse. Then read the others I've marked."

She sat with her back propped against one of the massive ponderosas, oblivious to all save the words before her. Elliot was leading her down a path, she realized after reading rapidly through all the verses, then returning to read each one slowly. He was trying to lead her down a path toward reconciliation with God. Tears had formed as she read about the adulterous woman against whom no man would cast the first stone. "Neither do I condemn you," Jesus had said, and Claire wanted to believe. "Let not your heart be troubled, neither let it be afraid." How she longed to believe! She was told she could approach God with full assurance, because Jesus had cleansed her heart from all her guilt. How she prayed to believe!

For years she had not comprehended the reality of faith in the Son of God, for her heart and mind had been sealed within a locked box of fear and guilt. With unswerving persistence Elliot had pried loose the lid of that box, until now she was glimpsing a light so radiant, so joyful, that she could not comprehend it. Could it actually be possible that God did not want her to spend her life bowed down in penance and shame, denied the love of man, as well as His heavenly love because of the nature of her guilt?

When she heard her name being called she lifted her head with a start to see that evening shadows were creeping over their campsite and night was fast approaching. All through supper she sensed Elliot's watchful gaze, and she knew he was hoping she would share with him when they went on the night hike. Her appetite fled, so she merely picked at her food until Doug leaned over and told her if she didn't eat up he'd feed her himself.

The group was unnaturally quiet as they hiked

single-file up a path and to a sloping meadow where the heavens lay bared before their eyes. All around them the dark silhouettes of the mountains rose in silent majesty as if to remind them how small and insignificant they were compared to the awesome wonder of God's creation. Elliot clasped Claire's hand and in ringing tones quoted, " 'When I consider your heavens, the work of your fingers, the moon and the stars, which you have set in place, what is man that you are mindful of him . . . you made him a little lower than the heavenly beings and crowned him with glory and honor . . .' "

"Look at those mountains," Page whispered in hushed tones, "it's sort of hard *not*, to believe in God out here, isn't it?"

Elliot and Claire sat apart from the others, in total darkness except for the light of the stars and a quarter moon. A breeze rippled over the long, cool meadow grasses, whispering with the timeless message of nature and spreading the fragrant odors of the mountains in summer. The silence was profound, deep, as if each member was captured by the urgent need to commune one to one with nature—and with God.

Claire lifted her head toward heaven, closing her eyes, feeling the kiss of the wind brushing her cheeks. *God, if You are truly willing to listen to me, please take away this guilt . . . please free me to love this man beside me as he deserves to be loved. If I can be forgiven, let me feel it . . . please . . .*

With almost one accord they turned to each other, Claire lifting her arms in supplication even as Elliot was reaching for her. "I love you," he whispered as lightly and softly as the breeze as he held her tight. "I love you, Claire Gerard, designer of dream homes and dream of my heart."

Feeling safe and protected in the dark, Claire nevertheless felt streams of light pouring into her, around her, and her own heart melted and joined the

158

stream. She wanted to be closer, she wanted to let him know with every drop of blood in her body how much she loved him. How could she have ever been afraid?

Her hands savored the touch of his thick hair, as dark as the night, as cool as the grass; she stroked his back and shoulders, marveling at his strength and power and that he was still being so very gentle with her.

"Aren't you going to kiss me, Elliot?" Claire whispered into his ear.

"Ah, love," he groaned and laughed at the same time. "I think the spell of the Sierras has bewitched you completely. What has become of the shy, reserved woman who couldn't bear to let me stand close to her?"

"I think you transformed her," Claire hugged him, burying her head in his chest and reveling in the thundering of his heart beneath her ear. For a moment they stayed thus, Elliot's hand caressing her hair while his other clasped her to him. "Elliot," she finally murmured, "I'm trying—really trying to pray. Do you think God will listen?"

"He's always listened, Claire," Elliot responded tenderly. "You just couldn't hear His reply." His hands slid up and lifted her face so that he could kiss her trembling lips. "Trust in Him like you've learned to trust in me. I promise you'll feel the same feelings you're feeling right now, only intensified a thousand times more."

"I think if I magnified the way I feel right now any stronger I'd burst like one of those catherine wheel firecrackers on the Fourth of July." She could feel his chest shaking with laughter, and a slow, sweet smile spread across her face. *God, please don't take him away from me. I'm trying to listen. I'm trying to believe.*

"Hey, are we going to spend the night out here?"

Michael called out into the night, breaking the mood of tranquility and joy. "I'm about to freeze my backside off."

Elliot stood and helped Claire up, heaving a deep sigh. "It is getting pretty late," he called back with obvious regret. "But don't worry—there are other nights, and the scenery isn't going anywhere." He turned on his flashlight, signalling the others to do the same.

"Sometimes," Claire heard him mutter *sotto voce* as they joined the others, "darkness isn't so bad after all, is it?"

CHAPTER 11

ON THE WAY BACK TO CAMP Claire twisted her ankle. It wasn't serious, but painful enough that the men had to take turns carrying her. She was ribbed mercilessly the entire time, and calls of "Watch out, wilderness, here comes Claire!" rang out in a bantering chant as she feebly tried to defend her ineptitude.

Elliot applied cool compresses soaked in water from the creek, then wrapped the offending ankle in an elastic bandage. "You'll be fine in a day or so," he pronounced. "That is, if I chain you by your tent and have you escorted everywhere you go." He cocked his head to one side, a bright blue glimmer flaring to life in his eyes. "I'd enjoy escorting you to the creek for your bath, of course."

Claire looked up, her senses bursting into flames as she lost herself in the intensity of his love. "I never thought I would feel like this again," she mused in a wondering tone.

"You're referring, of course, to the pain in your ankle?" he teased. "Do you want me to rub it some more?"

Leaning over, he planted his hands on the ground on either side of Claire, his smile as brilliant as the sun. With breath-taking slowness his head lowered and he kissed her slowly, luxuriously, until an amused throat-clearing behind them brought them both back to earth.

"I see you're taking Page's advice on kissing hurts to make them better," Rob observed with his usual dry humor.

Elliot stood up and dusted his hands off, keeping his eyes on Claire. "Only if the victim has short, rumpled honey-colored hair and eyes that change color with her moods."

"I didn't think Doug was in the market for kisses, if I recall correctly. Besides, I didn't know he had been hurt."

They all burst into laughter, Elliot blew Claire a final kiss, then followed Rob off to help him tighten the lines to their food sacks.

Claire was unable to go on hikes for the next two days, and had to bathe with the Newman sisters. Amazingly enough, she found she didn't mind the restriction or the loss of privacy. They truly had all become a family, and feeling cared about and supported after the year of isolation after her move to California was balm to her soul. Doug had smuggled along a miniature chess set and spent hours teaching her the finer arts of the game. Phil talked with her more about his Christian experience, and even showed her the verses that pointed her down the road to accepting forgiveness and being restored to a right relationship with Jesus.

Donna and Page were listening in during one of these times, and although Page still looked by and large disinterested, Claire could see the dawning understanding in Donna's eyes. "Y'know," she mused around one of her inevitable wads of chewing gum, "I can sort of see what you guys have going for you with all this Jesus stuff. He was quite a guy, wasn't He?"

Sunday at dusk Elliot conducted a service of worship, and as he was praying Claire felt, for the first time in years, that God was speaking to her. Speaking with love and mercy instead of anger and judgment. Her heart was full, and when she opened her eyes and lifted her head she looked straight into Elliot's lovingly intense gaze. For a suspended moment the others receded and the Sierras vanished in a cloud of dazzling light, as she communicated without words the wonder she was feeling inside. They concluded the service by singing "For the Beauty of the Earth," and never had Claire had the urgent need to sing out the glory of God as she needed to sing now. Had she truly been forgiven? Was everything all right now?

Elliot announced the next morning that there would only be one hike that day—a four or five hour one back to the site where the bus had dropped them off to pick up the supplies for their last week. "Claire, of course, will be unable to go, and I'm afraid I'm reduced to asking for at least one volunteer to stay here with her—preferably two."

"I'll stay," Michael immediately put in. "I don't think I'm ready for another torture trip like we endured to get here."

Claire was thrown into immediate panic. "My ankle's fine, Elliot. I can make it, I promise. Don't make anyone stay here on my account, please."

"Donna and I will stay with her," Page volunteered almost at the same time all of the others piped in their offers.

Elliot raised a commanding hand, shaking his head in rueful resignation. "I would have thought a week would have toughened up your tender feet and soft bodies. I can see now I'll have to come up with a system to decide who goes and who stays. I'll need at least seven to go so nobody will be overburdened with supplies." He smiled down at a still shaken Claire. "Trouble. That's all you are, lady. I knew it the first time I laid eyes on you and you wanted to come after me with a two-by-four . . ."

Diverted, Claire gaped at him. "I did not!"

"I wish you guys could have seen her," Elliot continued unabashed. "She was all set to defend this house she had designed with whatever it took—and in her case all it took was a pair of spitting mad green eyes and a voice that would slice through concrete."

"Elliot . . ." Claire buried her face in her hands while Doug playfully slapped her back and the others laughed.

"Be that as it may, I still have to come up with an equitable solution as to who stays with Calamity Claire."

"Why don't you just draw straws?" Donna suggested eagerly. "My sisters and I used to do it all the time to see who got the bathroom first."

No better solution was forthcoming, and nine sticks were quickly gathered and broken into appropriate lengths. When all were drawn, it turned out to be Donna, Rob—and Michael. There were various taunts of "You cheated!" and extravagant offers to trade, and no one but Elliot noticed Claire's sudden stillness, or the fact that her face had gone pale. He moved in front of her and squatted down.

"Don't worry—you're going to be safe—and undisturbed," he promised her gently, though there was a ring of steel in his voice. "Trust me, okay?"

She could only stare up at him and paste a brave smile on her face. "I do trust you, Elliot. With all my heart. "It's . . . it's others I have a problem with."

"I know." He paused. "Do you love me with all your heart as well?"

"You know I do."

"Good." He clapped his hands together and nimbly rose. "Okay, folks, the seven lucky ones who get to accompany me can go and get your packs ready. Be sure to pack lunch and snack foods, and plenty to drink. We leave in fifteen minutes." He waited until they had gone before turning to the remaining three.

"I don't like having to do this," he stated flatly. "I've never had to leave beginners alone for this long, but we've got to have those supplies or we'll be out of food before morning." A brief smile flitted across his stern countenance. "Of course, I've never had anyone quite like Claire come on my beginner's treks before. She definitely holds the record for the most mishaps." He captured her gaze in a warm study for a moment before focusing back on the others.

"I'll be leaving my spare radio behind. Rob, you're in charge of that. If anything happens you get in touch with me at once. I'll show you how to work it in a minute. However, as long as you remember everything I've told you, taught you these past weeks and months you should just be able to treat this day like any others, with a couple exceptions." He marked each of them in a light unsmiling glance. "No bathing, and no wandering out of camp."

"Aw, come on, Elliot," Michael protested. "We're not kids. Can't we at least hike around as long as we don't go too far?"

"Please, Elliot," Donna chimed in. "We all know our way around. There's nothing to *do* if we just have to sit around camp all day long waiting for you to get back. We'll be careful—we promise."

The corner of Elliot's mouth lifted. "You might not be children, but you sound just like them right now." He sighed, closed his eyes and bowed his head as if lost in thought. The others remained still, as if they knew he was considering their request but would balk if they pushed further.

Claire held her breath, understanding his dilemma but hoping he would agree because it would keep Michael away from her. The responsibility must be crushing, she realized.

"All right." He spoke slowly, carefully. "As you say, you're all adults, and hopefully have enough sense to know your limitations, and have learned enough respect for nature by now not to test her compassion." He paused again, this time more significantly. "Because she doesn't have any." Flexing his shoulders almost wearily, he stuffed his hands in the hip pockets of his jeans and idly scuffed his hiking boot through the loose pineneedles.

"There is one other thing." His gaze fastened on Claire and held it. "Claire has grown a lot during the past few months, and especially this past week. In fact, she's grown so much she's virtually emerged from her suffocating cocoon into a beautiful, freed butterfly." He grinned as Claire rolled her eyes and Michael snorted. "I'd sure hate for anything to happen that would send her fleeing back into that cocoon." With the startling swiftness of a swooping hawk his eyes fastened on Michael. "I trust you will all bear that in mind and act accordingly. If I come back and find her without the smile and new air of peace I've watched settle on her . . . I will not be pleased." He drawled the last words out, his voice going soft and so dangerous Claire had to suppress a shiver.

Michael flushed, glanced sideways at Claire, and then away. "I'm not going to do anything," he affirmed in a defensive tone, muttering an imprecation beneath his breath. "I just planned to explore around, take a nap."

"I'll keep him occupied," Donna moved to Michael's side and thrust her arm through his, pouting prettily up at him. "He won't be bored, Elliot."

"And I'll keep Claire company," Rob spoke up then, his expression reassuring both Claire and Elliot. "Don't worry, Elliot. We'll all do fine. Better, I assure you, than if we'd had to come on that hike."

Elliot stopped by Claire's tent before they left.

"Promise me you won't try anything beyond breathing, honey, okay?" He lifted her into his arms, hugged her tightly, then kissed her breathless so she couldn't even obey his teasing dictum. "I don't like leaving you like this, but I don't have a choice."

"I'll be fine, Elliot." She touched his lips, marveling at how she could hold and touch him so easily, marveling more at the love shining forth from his eyes. She had done nothing to deserve him—she didn't deserve him.

"Stop it, love," he kissed the fingers poised above his mouth. "You're worrying again—I can tell it because your eyes have gone brown, and you've got that forlorn look that makes me want to don my armor and slay all the demons snapping and snarling at your heart." He dropped a soft, benedictory kiss on her forehead. "Better yet, why don't you don the armor of God and then you won't need me to slay anything: you'll be equipped to do it yourself, with Christ."

"You're so sure of yourself, of your faith. Will I ever be that way?"

He held her arms, and a look of such intense agony went washing over his features Claire's heart went cold. "You've *got* to be," he replied fervently, desperately, "for the love of God—and for my love—you've got to be."

It was a long day. Claire and Rob chatted in desultory fashion for awhile, wandered around the campsite until Claire's weak ankle started aching, then sat and played with Doug's chess set which he had offered with a wink and a flourish.

Claire worked on her houseplan, which had developed now to a point where she could work on a watercolor rendering when she returned to Pacific Grove. She knew it was the best, the most unique and beautiful home she had ever designed, but there was little chance it would ever be built. Elliot had never made any mention of future plans together, and she could not imagine seeing this house built for anyone else.

With a wistful sigh she folded up the sheets of graph paper and stuffed them carefully in her backpack. Even if she wanted to sell the plan, she couldn't. The house had at least 4500 square feet, and Claire was not licensed to sell designs that size. What would Elliot think of it? Her face grew hot as she imagined his reaction, then dreamy as her mental musings turned to fantasies.

Lord . . . are You listening? You're supposed to know the desires of my heart, Josie said yesterday. Are You really not angry with me for dreaming about a life with Elliot? She looked up, up into the shimmering blue bowl of a sky, trying to listen, trying not to feel afraid and guilty. "I believe, Lord," she whispered aloud. "Please—please help my unbelief!"

Donna and Michael had disappeared from sight for most of the day, although every now and then Claire could hear their voices, and once she heard Michael yelling for Donna to come over where he was. They spotted the returning trekkers first and ran to meet them, flaunting their fit, relaxed states compared to the staggering, laden members.

"We did a lot better, though," Page announced when she shrugged out of her pack and collapsed on the ground. "Elliot only had to stop once this time."

Elliot had immediately shed his own pack and come over to Claire, his face perspiring freely and lined with concern even though he was smiling.

"I'm alive and well," Claire told him. "Not even a twinge in my ankle."

He led her off from the others, toward his tent. "Did you miss me half as much as I missed you?" he queried, taking her hand and swinging it between them.

"Nope."

He stopped, looking down at her with a ferocious scowl. "Explain yourself, woman."

"I missed you twice as much—Elliot!"

She squealed as he picked her up and swung her around and around. They laughed together, trying to clear away the dizziness. Suddenly, all Claire's niggling questions and doubts scattered like a flock of birds startled into flight.

After supper that night Elliot complimented the members who had stayed behind, thanking them for obeying instructions. He also complimented the ones who had acted as pack mules, as Phil had teasingly called them, reminding them that it was due to their superb conditioning since he had taken over their lives.

The last week of Nature's Journeymen Trek IIB should have been idyllic. It turned into a nightmare.

CHAPTER 12

CLAIRE PLEADED TO BE allowed to go on the hikes the following day, but after Elliot tested her ankle and saw her wince his answer was an unequivocal "no." Since the group would only be gone a little over an hour, he let her stay by herself, although Claire could tell when they returned that his mind had been back here at the camp instead of with the other members. He was also looking tired, somehow strained, and Claire had to bite her tongue to keep from asking what was wrong. She was afraid of what the answer might be, so she kept her worry to herself.

After their afternoon hike Elliot disappeared into his tent. Claire was sitting propped against a tree making a stack of pinecones when Donna plopped down beside her.

"I wish you could have been with us this time," she said, her voice excited. "We found a badger trapped on a ledge and Elliot rescued him."

"It was something," Brad added. He and Phil had wandered over to join them and now they all began to tell Claire the saga. Elliot had used the coil of nylon rope he kept in his pack, fashioning a loop and after phenomenal patience and skill managing to snag it around the frightened badger's middle. Instructing all the others to move out of sight behind a nearby outcropping of rock, he slowly drew the snapping, snarling animal up, and was barely able to retrieve the rope before the badger tore off into the surrounding woods.

"He looked pretty skinned up, but couldn't have been too badly injured or he never could have disappeared that fast," Phil ended. He and Brad turned as Doug hailed them, and they loped back to the middle of the camp.

"Elliot was marvelous," Donna sighed. She looked at Claire enviously. "He sure is gone over you, isn't he? Some gals have all the luck."

Claire colored, but ignored her observation. "Well, I sure wish I could have been there," she stated, the wistfulness undisguised. "Was it too far away from camp?"

Donna's eyes lit up. "Hey—what a good idea! It's not that far—you want me to take you and at least show you the ledge? Are you sure your ankle's okay?"

"It's fine as long as I don't put any pressure on it the wrong way." Restlessness and a surge of frustrated longing surged through her. "Do you think it would be all right if we went? I suppose I ought to ask Elliot if it's out of earshot."

Donna airily waved her hand. "Oh, that's not necessary. Didn't we prove the other day we can take care of ourselves without him nursemaiding our every step? Besides, he's crashed in his tent, sound asleep." She stood up. "Tell you what, I'll ask Mike to come with us. It's always more fun with a man, huh?" She hurried on as she saw Claire's doubtful expression. "Oh, he won't bother you anymore, Claire. Since Elliot all but branded you with his name Michael turned to more—shall we say—willing prospects?"

171

She smiled a creamy, secret smile and helped Claire rise to her feet. "Come on, it's plain you're bored out of your skull. It'll be fun, and we'll be back in an hour. Elliot won't even know we've gone."

Claire followed her slowly over to Michael's tent. She knew she ought to let Elliot know, but she hated to wake him if he was asleep. His eyes had looked so shadowed the last day or so, and although he was in superb condition no body could function as well without proper rest. Donna was right. If it was only a short distance from camp there was really no reason to make such a fuss about it. They'd managed fine on their own the other day, they had been out here for ten days now and were all more conversant with wilderness living. And it would be so marvelous to finally stretch her legs and her lungs again.

They left a few minutes later. Donna assured Claire that she had left word with the Newman sisters where they were going. "Just like Elliot made us promise," she pointed out to Claire smugly. "They'll know where we are even if we will be back before anyone knows we've gone."

"You sure you can make it, Claire? I don't fancy being wiped all over the side of a mountain if you turn your delicate little ankle all over again." Michael smiled to show he was joking, but there was an underlying sting beneath the words. Claire wondered if he was still miffed about her lack of response to his overtures.

She soon forgot doubts and traces of uneasiness and awkwardness as she was led down a narrow path, across a meadow covered in lupine, and into a dense stretch of forest. It was so quiet she could hear her own breathing, and although she had to step carefully she was still able to relax and unwind in the wild serenity of her surroundings.

"We have to go over an outcropping of rocks, remember?" Michael warned a few minutes later.

"Was it to the left or right when we came out of this part of the woods?"

"Left, I think," Donna replied. She glanced back over her shoulder at Claire. "You doing okay?"

"Fine, but is it very much further? It seems like we've been walking an awful long time."

"Don't be such a worry wart. It's right beyond the outcropping of rocks. We'll show you and then head back." Michael's voice was studded with impatience. Claire bit her lip and resolved not to say another word.

They seemed to pick their way along a nonexistent trail forever before finally coming upon the rocky hillside. It looked as if some giant had carelessly dumped a load of crushed rock, and Claire caught her breath. The way was precipitous, with few handholds or even the hint of a trail for their feet.

"Donna," she ventured at last, trying to keep her voice from reflecting her growing worry, "are you sure you know where we're going?"

Donna laughed a high, alarmingly uncertain laugh. "It does seem like it's taking longer than it did before," she admitted.

Michael turned back, stopping abruptly and swearing when his foot slipped on a pile of loose stone. "You stupid fool," he grated, "what are you going to do if we're lost? None of this looks familiar—I thought you said you knew where it was."

Donna hung her head, dashing a suddenly trembling hand across her brow. "I've just been following you, Michael. I haven't recognized anything since we left the woods."

They stared at each other in growing horror. Claire gingerly lowered herself onto a rock and took off her backpack. "Well, why don't we try to retrace our steps?" she suggested as calmly as she could. "It shouldn't be too hard."

"Right." Michael savagely gestured with one hand. "Go ahead. Which way?"

Claire looked back in the general direction from where they had come. There was no sign, no unusual markings to help lead them: all she saw was a jumbled mass of increasingly dangerous rock and a few scattered green bushes. None of it was familiar in spite of the fact that they had hiked over it only a few moments before. She quailed inwardly, but refused to allow the fear to take hold. Panic, Elliot had hammered into their heads, was the worst enemy of anyone lost in the mountains.

"Does *any* of it look familiar?" she asked after a moment when neither Donna or Michael seemed to be doing anything beyond glaring at one another in frustration.

"I think we should have turned right back there instead of left," Donna admitted in a small voice, huddling down when Michael blistered her with a few choice phrases.

Claire felt all her old fears rising at his show of anger and frustration, but she also felt sorry for Donna, who was looking close to tears. "Let's eat a snack." She rummaged in her pack without waiting and dug out a granola bar.

They crunched in silence for a few minutes, and Claire struggled to remember everything that Elliot had told them. Don't panic, conserve your energy, take stock of your surroundings . . .

"I'm going to climb up to the top of this outcropping," Michael interrupted her mental instructions abruptly. "Maybe I can see where we are and figure out which way to head."

"I'll come with you," Donna scrambled up, taking hold of his arm and looking at him pleadingly.

"Oh, all right," Michael gave in grudgingly. "Will you be all right here, Claire? We'll come back and get you in a few minutes."

"Try not to take too long. It's going to be dark in less than two hours."

"I know." He cursed, and began climbing the side of the slope, Donna at his heels.

I won't panic, Claire ordered herself over and over. I won't panic. I'll think of Elliot, and how much I love him. I'll think of how much he says he loves me. Will he worry? Will he wake up and know we're missing? Thank heavens Donna had told the Newman sisters where they were headed so if worse came to worse Elliot would know where to start searching. Maybe she should try to pray. *Lord, here I am again. Do You hear me? I'm a little bit scared. I wish I knew some more Bible verses I could quote about now . . .*

A sudden breeze lifted her damp hair, and on the tail of it the thought suddenly went winging through her brain. 'I lift up my eyes to the hills . . . My help comes from the Lord.' With widening eyes she gazed up into the sky, her heart beating in a thudding, irregular rhythm. 'Perfect love drives out fear . . .' 'Though I walk through the valley . . . I will fear no evil, for You are with me.'

God? Oh, God thank You! You do care for me, You do! You have all along. You've cared for me and loved me and—forgiven me! It doesn't have to be a sad song I sing, does it, Lord? You're with me all the time, day or night, and the songs I can sing can always be full of praise and triumph, can't they? That's what the psalmist meant in my Psalm—because You led Your people safely through the wilderness he could ultimately trust in Your power, in the promise of Your love. All those years of guilt and loneliness and despair You were still there, weren't You, waiting for me to turn around and take Your hand. Father, get us back to camp, please. I must share this with Elliot, I must tell him You have lifted me back up into Your arms again. That verse in John, Lord! That verse Phil read the other day about being sheep and Jesus will never let us go—it makes sense now!

175

Tears of joy and release were bleeding down her cheeks, and she was so exultant she stood up, clasping her hands together in reverential praise. I'm free, she wanted to shout to the mountains, to the air. *Praise God, I'm free to love You and free to give my love to Elliot. Free to receive whatever love he chooses to give to me. I can't wait—*

The scream was sharp, shrill and so shocking Claire could not credit its reality. Her head jerked around to stare up the rock-strewn hillside, eyes dilating in horror when another scream bounced and echoed throughout the late afternoon. It was Donna, and she was screaming Michael's name, and then Claire's.

With shaking fingers she quickly strapped on her pack, keeping her eyes glued to the far-off top of the slope. Her breath came in short, sharp stabs and after only three steps her ankle throbbed in protest, but Claire ignored the pain in her body. Scrambling desperately for holds, she found her way up the steep, unfriendly slope, scraping her palms, bumping her shins, but she made it up the slope.

Donna was hysterical, weeping in loud, uncontrollable sobs. She was kneeling at the edge of a precipice, and Claire's blood ran cold. She started to run over to her, staggered as her ankle gave way, and limped until she dropped beside the prostrate young woman.

"Donna, where's Michael?" Her voice was urgent, shaking from exertion and fear.

"I didn't mean to do it—it was an accident! Oh, God, what if he's dead? It's my fault, it's all my fault!" She moaned and wept, the crying accelerating back upwards to keening screams.

Claire took hold of her shoulders and shook her. "Donna, get hold of yourself and tell me where he is."

"He fell!" she sobbed, pointing a violently trembling finger down. "He tripped because of me and fell over the edge!" She stared up with the vacant stare of an insane person, her eyes red and streaming tears, mouth slack and quivering uncontrollably. "Claire, . . . I've killed Michael."

"You don't know that!" Claire interrupted harshly, her throat aching with tension. She flopped down onto her stomach and inched her way over until she could peer down, and what she saw caused her to close her eyes as a wave of faintness threatened to engulf her. Michael had fallen about fifteen feet, mercifully onto a large slab jutting outwards. He wasn't moving. "But that doesn't mean he's dead," Claire whispered to herself in an impassioned, choked little voice. "That doesn't mean he's dead."

She wiggled back, sat up, and turned to Donna. "Donna! You've *got* to stop crying and help me. Donna!" Her own control fraying when there was no response, she finally took a deep breath, closed her eyes a moment, then slapped Donna across her cheek.

"Oh!" The sobs caught in her throat, and Donna looked at Claire in stunned amazement.

"I'm sorry," Claire choked. "But we've got to work together and I can't do anything if you keep having hysterics."

"But I killed him," she repeated in a pathetic litany.

"We don't know that!" Claire snapped back. "A ledge broke his fall. He's about fifteen feet down. One of us needs to get down there to check him while the other starts a signal fire at the highest point of this hill."

"I can't go down there!" Her voice was panicked, and tears spurted afresh from her eyes. "I can't, Claire! I just can't. I might fall! It's all my fault!"

Claire stared numbly at her lacerated palms, then experimentally wriggled her ankle. The pain was excruciating, but how must Michael feel—if he could feel at all? "All right, Donna, I'll climb down to Michael, but you *must* start a fire. Do you understand? We have to try and help Elliot find us.'' Once again she took Donna by her shoulders, holding her until the other girl jerkily nodded through her tears. ''Make sure you surround it with stones and stay out of those trees. Use as many dead leaves and bushes as you can to create a lot of smoke.''

Thank You, Lord, for bringing all this to mind. Thank You for Elliot, too.

There was not time to linger. Already shadows were lengthening and the sun was turning to flaming orange, descending with frightening speed behind the chain of mountains in front of them. Claire searched frantically through their packs for anything she could use as bandages. She found a Nature's Journeymen T-shirt in Michael's and a sweater in Donna's, and wrapped them about her waist without a flicker of regret. She stuffed half the food and two canteens in her own backpack, took a deep unsteady breath, and approached the edge once more.

You know when sparrows fall, she reminded God with half-hysterical humor, *but I do hope You will see fit to keep one of Your restored children from doing so.*

Donna was moving with stumbling steps, still sobbing loudly as she gathered stones and kindling. Claire spared her one last wave as she prepared to ease herself down the ledge. Only God Himself knew the extent of her terror, but it was over surprisingly fast. Claire decided extreme fear blanked out the awareness of time, and was grateful.

She would never be able to recall how she made it down to Michael. She would remember the deathlike calmness as she slithered and slid, the stinging pain as her already abused body suffered further, and finally the paralyzing relief when she was beside Michael and could see the rise and fall of his chest. He was alive. She spared a second to bow her head and thank God, and then felt him with hands shaking so badly she almost smiled. His leg was twisted beneath him so awkwardly she was certain it was broken, and the back of his head was matted with blood, swollen where he must have hit it. But he was alive. Now all she had to do was pray that Elliot would be able to find them.

CHAPTER 13

SHE WAS AMAZED AT THE EASE with which she could touch Michael, a man for whom she had felt wariness and fear. She splashed a little water from the canteen to wipe away as much of the blood on his head as she could, then used the folded T-shirt as a pillow. His leg was another matter. If she tried to move him to a more comfortable position she might make bad matters worse, even sever a nerve or artery since she didn't know how bad the break was.

Dear Lord, please let Elliot find us soon. She covered him with Donna's sweater and then collapsed against the side of the mountain, allowing herself a few moments of tears and trembling while she faced their predicament.

Michael stirred, groaning as his lids fluttered and fell. Claire moved instantly to his side. "Lie still, Michael," she commanded him firmly. "You have a broken leg and a bad cut on the back of your head. You must be still."

"My head . . ." he moaned, stirring a little and then emitting a gasp of pain. "My leg . . . what happened?'' He tried to turn his head, but Claire put a desisting hand on it, then moved so he could see her.

"Try to relax," she spoke as calmly as she could, then repeated what had happened to him. His eyes were glassy from shock and pain, and she could see the pulse in his neck palpitating far too rapidly. *Help, Lord.*

"Claire?'' Her name was slurred, feeble, and his hand moved out blindly to touch her knee where it rested near his head. "Claire, I hurt." He struggled to withhold another moan, perspiration breaking out across his brow. "Where's . . . Donna?"

"Lighting a signal fire. Help will be here soon. You just try and relax."

"Wha–what . . . happened?"

"You fell, Michael. Please stop talking and rest." Her voice cracked, and she bit her lip. Her knowledge of first aid had been limited to bandaging Gary's myriad cuts and scrapes after one of his binges. What would she do if Michael went into shock?

"Hurts," he mumbled, moving fretfully. "Claire . . . I hurt . . ." the words faded away into a groaning mumble, and she saw him shiver suddenly.

With no thought beyond trying to keep him still she reached and lifted his hand between her own and held it tightly. "Shh . . . you must keep quiet, Michael. Elliot will be here soon. I know he will."

His eyes opened painfully. "Want to apologize, Claire."

She gaped at him. "What on earth are you talking about, Michael? No—please don't tell me—just rest. Rest."

His hand moved within her hold, turning to squeeze back weakly. "I'm sorry for the way I treated you. Had no right . . . will you . . . forgive me?"

"I forgive you, Michael." She gently loosed one of her hands and tenderly caressed his brow. She knew what it felt like to feel unforgiven. "Please don't worry about it anymore. It isn't important."

The merest nuance of a grin touched his pain-thinned mouth. "Elliot's a lucky guy."

Tears pricked her lids. "I'm a lucky woman," she replied in turn, and for a few moments there was silence.

"Claire . . ." Michael murmured feebly after awhile, his hand gripping hers so tightly she winced. "Would you mind . . . would it bother you to—to hold me?" He gasped as his agitation caused him to involuntarily move his leg. "I'm a little cold, and—and—sort of stupid to admit—I'm scared."

Claire's heart twisted within, for she knew instinctively what it must have cost a man like Michael to make such an admission.

"It won't bother me at all," she told him gently. With careful movements she managed to ease his head into her lap, not even noticing the oozing blood that seeped through onto her jeans. She soothed light fingers over his brow with one hand, while the other clasped his hand.

Michael sighed. "Thanks. You're quite a woman, Claire. . . . " His voice faded away and in a few moments he had drifted into unconsciousness.

Claire sat there holding him, part of her absently noting her own multitude of aches and pains, but the greater part was singing a song of triumph. She was holding him without fear, without disgust. She was caring for him with the compassion of Christ filling her heart, giving her a strength she never dreamed she could possess. "Elliot, look at me," she wanted to shout. "I'm whole now. Let me give you my love, my life."

Lord, please, please send him to get us off this ledge and back home in safety.

She looked up when she heard Donna calling her name. The other girl was still crying, but at least the hysterics had abated a little.

"I got a fire going!" she said, the tears still

thickening her voice. "Claire, is he—" she choked, unable to go on.

"He's got a broken leg and he's cut his head, but I think he'll be okay," Claire called back up to her, trying to pitch her voice low enough to keep from waking Michael. "You tend the fire."

"What if no one comes? What if we're stranded here forever? We'll die." Her voice started to rise again. "It's all my fault. *My* fault!"

"Donna, please. Blaming yourself won't do anyone any good. Just keep that fire going—and pray."

"What's the use? God doesn't care about us. I haven't been to church in years. Besides, it's all my fault . . ."

"God will hear." Claire savored the peace that filled her heart, the new assurance of His heavenly care. "He hears us, Donna."

"Then tell Him to get us off this mountain!" Donna screamed, breaking down anew and turning away from the ledge.

Claire listened as her cries faded, and she prayed desperately that Donna would maintain enough presence of mind to keep the fire burning. The sun was sinking fast.

She was nodding, fighting drowsiness, exhaustion, and growing pain when she heard the voices. She stared first down at Michael, but though he had occasionally groaned and muttered he hadn't regained consciousness. Then who—?

"Claire!" Elliot was peering over the edge, and Claire looked up in relief.

"Elliot," she breathed, and her face was transformed with joy. "I knew you would come."

"Are you okay?" Even as he was talking he was unwrapping a coil of rope. On either side of him Phil's and Doug's heads appeared, their faces dark with anxiety. There was a sound of metal against stone, and then the rope uncoiled and fell almost at Michael's feet. Elliot rappelled down and then he was beside her.

He helped Claire ease Michael's head off her lap, examined him with swift but thorough skill, then turned to Claire. For a suspended moment they stared at one another in the fading twilight. "Claire," he whispered, and then she was in his arms.

He kissed her mouth, her eyes, her temples, his hands running over her body as if he couldn't believe she was really there, and all in one piece. Claire could only cling, her legs so weak he was holding her up. She tried to tell him about Michael, about Donna, about what had happened, and that she had met her Lord. The words got all tangled up in tears and kisses, though, until Elliot pulled her hard against him and hugged her so tightly she couldn't speak at all, much less breathe.

"I'm never letting you out of my sight again," he muttered fiercely against her hair. "Never! And I just might kill the next person that leads you astray like this."

Claire pulled her head away from its comforting nest against his shoulder and laid her palm over his mouth. "I should have asked you first," she told him. "But you were asleep, and Donna said we'd be back in an hour. But we all should have known better, Elliot. Please don't frown so. You frighten me."

He took her hand, examined it and let out a harsh, shuddering breath. "I frighten myself," he confessed, sweeping a sweat-matted lock of hair from her face. "The feelings I've gone through in the last two hours don't bear repeating." He took a deep breath, glancing up to Doug and Phil and giving them a thumbs-up sign. "Now, let's get you off this ledge and pray the chopper will make it before dark."

He tied the rope around her waist and gently slid the gloves he had shoved in his back pocket over her hands. "Just hold onto the rope," he instructed, "and

Doug and Phil will do the rest." He paused, gazing at her a minute and Claire saw, incredibly, tears swimming in the depths of his turbulent gray-blue eyes. "God, thank You for watching over her," he whispered, his gaze never leaving her stunned face. "Claire . . . I love you."

"And I love you." The first real smile she had shed all day broke across her ravaged, filthy countenance. She was still smiling when she was hauled over the top of the cliff and into Doug's arms.

"Boy, Claire, you're in for it now," Phil shook his head, then leaned back over the edge to ask Elliot about Michael.

Doug hugged Claire, then helped her to the ground as her legs gave way completely.

"You really okay?" Doug asked, and she nodded.

"Except for my ankle." She tried to turn it and grimaced. "I guess that last slide down to Michael was more than it could handle, but I must confess I've had about all the hiking I care to do, this week anyway."

Amid the relieved laughter came the sound of wings beating the air, and seconds later the last rays of the sun glinted off the metal frame of the chopper fast approaching from the south. With incredible ease it landed on a fairly level spot about a hundred feet away, and two men hopped out with a stretcher.

Donna had crept over to Claire while Michael was being hauled up from the ledge, her eyes huge, liquid. She wasn't crying anymore, but there was a look of utter despair clouding her face, an aura of bleak melancholy that not even their rescue could penetrate. She sprang to life when the two men carrying Michael on the stretcher passed them on their way back to the chopper.

"Is he going to be all right?" she asked, her voice quavery.

"He'll be fine," one of the medics assured her.

They stopped and lowered the stretcher to let her see, and Donna knelt by its side, her hand stealing out to touch Michael's face. His eyes fluttered open.

"Michael," she choked. "I'm sorry."

He managed a ghost of a grin. "S'okay. Don't worry, Donna ... come visit me in the hospital, okay?" His eyes closed, and the medic touched Donna's arm.

"Let us go now. He's going to be all right, I promise."

"But it's all my fault," Donna burst out, sobs starting afresh. "How can he want to see me again?"

They had all come up to her now, and Phil put his arms around Donna and drew her away as they watched the men load Michael in the chopper and fly off into the sunset. "Doubtless because he knows you didn't do it on purpose," he told her gently, "and because he *wants* to see you again."

"I don't understand," Donna repeated, shaking her head. "I just don't understand ..."

They spent the night there on top of the mountain, beneath the small stand of sugar pines. Elliot had warned the other members they probably wouldn't try to hike back to camp, and had radioed Rob after everyone was settled.

"*They* all know to stay put," he remarked pointedly after over-and-outing. Wrapping an arm around Claire, he balled his other fist and gently chucked her chin. "I trust you and Donna have learned your lesson?"

"Most assuredly, Mr. Ramsey," Claire promised, mouth curving into a smile when his fist unfolded and his fingers clasped her chin. "Are you going to extract a suitable punishment for our crimes?"

"It would serve you right if you were both stuck with cooking and cleaning up the rest of the week."

"Elliot ..." Donna's voice came hesitantly out of

the dark, "Can you ever forgive me for being so dumb?"

They were all sitting huddled together around the remains of the fire, which Elliot had just extinguished before everyone retired to sleeping bags for the night. Donna had been withdrawn, almost zombie-ish, doing what she was asked to do and saying little unless she was spoken to directly. Claire suddenly experienced the strangest sense of *déjà vu,* as if she were watching an old movie reel of—herself.

"Of course I do, Donna." Elliot's voice was very gentle. "I can't deny that I was very angry with all of you when I woke up to find out what you'd done, but I'm certainly not going to carry the anger to my grave." He drew Claire closer to his side and began idly stroking her cheek, throat, and the slope of her shoulder. "The Bible tells us not to let the sun go down on our anger, and there's a very sound reason for that. Negative feelings like anger—and guilt— destroy people from the inside out. Take Claire here."

"I think you've already got her," Doug inserted across from them, and Claire made a rude noise.

Elliot hushed her with a brief kiss. "When I first met Claire, she was wrapped in fear, the fear she was carrying around and after I took her out a few times it was also easy to see she was carrying a sackload of guilt so heavy her natural personality was suffocating. And it's all so unnecessary."

"Anyone who has accepted Christ as Savior learns they were forgiven two thousand years ago, when He died such a horrible death on the cross." Claire spoke with a tranquility and assurance that was music to Elliot's ears, and she knew it from the sudden acceleration she could feel in his heart beating next to her ear. "Donna, remember when I shared with you all about my husband?"

"He must have been a jerk. So what does that have to do with anything?" Her voice was bewildered.

187

"I blamed myself for his death. For years I had prayed—prayed, Donna, that God would take Gary out of my life. I wasn't thinking in terms as final as death; I just wanted to be rid of him. When he died I just knew it was my fault."

"That doesn't make any sense. How could it be your fault?"

Claire smiled in the darkness. There had been a little bit of life in Donna's voice then. *Please, Lord, help her to see as You helped me.*

"I was afraid of my husband, then I hated him. I could have tried to understand, helped him to seek help. Instead I only wanted to be rid of him." She searched for Elliot's hand and grasped it tightly. "And so in a sense it *was* my fault. But I was wrong to turn my back on God and think He had turned His back on me, when all along all I had to do was ask forgiveness—and then accept it."

"Tell me, Donna," Elliot inserted, "did you mean to trip Michael and cause him to fall?"

"Oh, no!" Donna gasped. "No—it was an accident. I swear it was—"

"Easy, easy," Elliot soothed. "And didn't Michael forgive you in spite of the fact that you did *accidentally* cause him to fall?"

There was a long pause. "Well . . . I guess."

"Then don't you see it's the same kind of situation as Claire faced? She couldn't ask her dead husband to forgive her for her feelings, but she could ask God to forgive her, and accept the fact that He does—and always will. All you need to do is accept Michael's forgiveness, and mine. Don't feel guilty anymore, Donna."

"Why don't you let me show you a few passages from the New Testament that explain how you can accept forgiveness, Donna?" Phil put in, moving over to sit beside Donna and engage her in a soft, earnest conversation.

"Claire and I are going to go look at the moon," Elliot whispered softly to Doug, and a soft chuckle followed them as he lifted her into his arms and carried her out from beneath the trees.

There with the moon shimmering in silvery white splendor, so close you could pluck it out of the sky, Elliot let her slide down to her feet, being careful to hold her so she wasn't resting any weight on her ankle as he cupped her face between his hands.

"You really do understand, don't you?" he questioned, the joy and relief evident in his husky voice.

"I was sitting alone while I waited for Michael and Donna," she whispered back in a voice just as husky, "wishing I could remember more Bible verses and all of a sudden there they were, crowding into my mind so fast I didn't have time to be afraid."

She worshiped him with her eyes, lovingly tracing the thick eyebrows, the lean cheeks, his beard-roughened jaw. In the moonlight his eyes reflected a molten silver so liquid, so deep, that she could have drowned in its depths. "Just before Donna screamed it hit me—Jesus loves me just as I am, in spite of all those horrible feelings I felt, in spite of everything, He loved me and forgave me and died for me."

"If you only knew how I've prayed to hear you say those words." His voice was choked. "How could I ask you to marry me and be my wife if you couldn't free yourself from the past?"

Claire went very still. "Elliot," she murmured in burgeoning hope, in incredulous joy, "does that mean you're asking me now?"

"Not right this minute, no." His mouth covered hers in a searing kiss. "I was going to kiss you under this moon for awhile and then ask you."

"Oh!" she gasped in helpless relief and laughter. "In that case, my answer is no right now."

"Hmmm . . . I guess I'll have to try and change your mind." He spent the next several minutes doing so quite effectively, until he managed to put a few inches between them, though he was holding her hands in his strong ones.

"Ah, my most precious love," he whispered, resting his cheek on her head while they caught their breath and struggled to still their clamoring senses. "I've been waiting for you all my life, and the last few months it seems as if my life has lasted forever."

He hugged her suddenly. "Claire—let's thank God here, now, for what He has done for us, and ask His blessing on our marriage."

"I'd like to do that very much, Elliot," Claire answered on a bubble of laughter, "but we can't. You still haven't asked me to marry you yet."

"I did say you were turning into a flirt, didn't I?" Elliot murmured dryly. "I can see now I'm going to have my hands full."

With loving tenderness he placed his hands on either side of her face, turning her so her face was bathed in moonlight. "Claire Gerard, will you marry me?"

"I thought you'd never ask!" She fell back into his arms, tears of happiness trickling down her face to be lovingly swept away by Elliot. "Elliot, I do love you so much, and just pray that I can truly be the kind of Christian wife you need."

"A helper suitable for me," he quoted softly. "You became that when you became reconciled to the Lord, honey. Let's pray now."

And there with the moon streaming down and bathing them in its flow, with the Sierras surrounding them and the wind blowing around them, they committed their lives to each other, and to God.

"Can we tell everyone?" Claire asked as Elliot carried her back toward their makeshift camp a long time later.

"My love, they've known since the first day they saw us together. I'm not very good at hiding how I feel about you, in case you haven't noticed."

"When can we get married?"

"As soon as possible?" They exchanged another loving kiss. "We can live in my apartment in Monterey until our home is built."

"Home is built?" Claire echoed, wondering if she should mention her plan.

"Yes." His thumb traced her mouth, slid to the pulse throbbing a deep rhythm in her neck. "The home you've been designing so beautifully these past two weeks. It's perfect, honey. Incredibly, wonderfully perfect and a dream design if I ever saw one."

"How—how did you know about it?" Even in the darkness with all problems cleared between them she still felt her face heating up. "I hadn't meant to let you see it."

"Well, we'll work on your self-confidence as a home designer married to an architect later." He dropped a kiss on the tip of her nose. "I found the sketch the day you tried to freeze yourself to death in the river. I'll confess now I've sneaked back in your tent to see how it was progressing several times when you were occupied elsewhere. My love, you have remarkable talent and imagination, did you know that?"

She reached up and tugged his head down. "I just love you," she murmured against his mouth.

"You can spend the next sixty or seventy years demonstrating that in between designing homes. How 'bout a partnership, madam dream designer? In every way."

"Elliot . . . I'm not *that* good, and I don't have an architectural degree, and—mmph." Her protests died beneath the onslaught of his kisses, and after awhile she decided it didn't matter anyway. She could, after all, design homes while he designed buildings and churches and malls. They would be a good team. "Elliot, there is one other thing . . ."

"What's that?"

191

"Would you mind if we had four bridesmaids and five groomsmen—if Michael is out of the hospital in time?"

The night rang with their laughter, and the shadows of the trees enfolded them, swallowing their figures up in darkness. Around them loomed the Sierras, majestic and still, their awesome silence a song eternally praising the almighty God.

ABOUT THE AUTHOR

Although her husband and family remain her first calling, SARA MITCHELL feels strongly that God has led her to a writing ministry. She says that "As each day passes I discover that I need to write like I need to breathe, because I have such a wonderful opportunity to share my faith." It is a joyful experience for her to be able to write not only about the ". . . way of a man with a maiden . . ." as God meant for it to be, but to write about the love of Christ as well.

A Letter to Our Readers

Dear Reader:

Welcome to the world of Serenade Books—a series designed to bring you the most beautiful love stories in the world of inspirational romance. They will uplift you, encourage you, and provide hours of wholesome entertainment, so thousands of readers have testified. In order that we might better contribute to your reading enjoyment, we would appreciate your taking a few minutes to respond to the following questions and return to:

Editor, Serenade Books
The Zondervan Publishing House
1415 Lake Drive, S.E.
Grand Rapids, Michigan 49506

1. Did you enjoy reading A SONG IN THE NIGHT?

   ☐ Very much. I would like to see more books by this author!
   ☐ Moderately
   ☐ I would have enjoyed it more if _____

   _____

2. Where did you purchase this book? _____

3. What influenced your decision to purchase this book?

   ☐ Cover   ☐ Back cover copy
   ☐ Title   ☐ Friends
   ☐ Publicity   ☐ Other _____

4. What are some inspirational themes you would like to see treated in future books?

_____

5. Please indicate your age range:
   ☐ Under 18   ☐ 25–34   ☐ 46–55
   ☐ 18–24   ☐ 35–45   ☐ Over 55

6. If you are interested in receiving information about our Serenade Home Reader Service, in which you will be offered new and exciting novels on a regular basis, please give us your name and address. (This does NOT obligate you for membership.)

Name _____

Occupation _____

Address _____

City _____ State _____ Zip _____

Serenade / Saga books are inspirational romances in historical settings, designed to bring you a joyful, heart-lifting reading experience.

Serenade / Saga books available in your local book store:

Serenade / Serenata books are inspirational romances in contemporary settings, designed to bring you a joyful, heart-lifting reading experience.

Serenade / Serenata books available in your local bookstore:

Watch for other books in both the *Serenade/Saga* (historical) and *Serenade/Serenata* (contemporary) series coming soon.